Thank you to my friends and family

Jeff, Janette, Amanda, and Alec

Your support means the world to me.

Special thanks to:

Designs by LM.

For my book cover and my designs

3

Raven Watters
Author

Titles by Raven Watters

Red Haze

Destiny's Divine Plan

Crazy for his Love

Wings of Desire

Thorns of Time

Table of Contents

Table of Contents

The End

Italics indicate dreams

Chapter One
Start of Fate

The impact of the car hitting us sent shards of glass sailing through the air. The slow motion of the scene made it seem unreal. My body moved to the side as my head hit the window. The glass shattered with the impact. The blood started to trickle down my forehead, into my eye. The pain sent swords through my entire being. The blood in my eye blurred my vision.

My mother's hair swung to the right, then the left as the impact made her imitate a ragdoll. The limb of the tree came into the passenger window next to my mother. She opened her mouth to scream, but no sound came out. The point of the branch entered my mother's chest from the side.

Dad was looking over at mom as his body was thrown toward then away from her. His eyes closed as the headlights from the vehicle shined into his face. His eyes glazed over as he reached for mom. He took her hand in his own. Mom gripped his hand tighter. Nothing from my dad. Mom stopped moving her hand.

I was stuck. I reached for my seatbelt as the glass dug into my hand. I tried to scream but no sound came out of my mouth. The headlights were so bright. I wanted the lights to shut off. The blood of my parents dripped from the headliner in the car. The drip came from the roof in slow motion as it landed on the top of my mom's hand, holding dad's. The seatbelt won't come undone.

I try to look down to undo the buckle. My head won't turn. Pain slices through my neck like a rusty, blunt knife. My right arm won't move. The car door is holding my arm between it and the seat. My heart beats faster as I work to get my arm unstuck. I fail to get my arm unstuck as a person appears in front of my eyes. "Are you okay? Can you hear me?" A soft male voice calms me.

I blink several times to clear my vision. I can't answer him. My voice is barely above a whisper. "I can't see you. My arm is stuck. I think there is something wrong with my neck. I am going to die. My mom and dad are dead. My heart is still beating but I know I'm going to die."

I sat straight up in my bed with the
sweat beads covering my face. Tears
streamed down my face as I realize I was
dreaming about the accident again. My
pillowcase was covered in sweat as I hit it
with disgust. My memories haunt me nearly
every night. I don't remember much after
that except that I woke up in the hospital.

"Natalie, time for breakfast."
Grandma yelled up the stairs to my
bedroom.

"On my way Nana. I am just waking
up." I rest my forehead against my arms

crossed over my knees that I had pulled up. I had gone a few years without any nightmares to haunt me, now all of the sudden, it's every night that they torment me. Haven't I had to relive that night enough? I blamed myself for them dying. Was this the cruelty of karma coming back to me? If I hadn't been out drinking with my friends on my eighteenth birthday, they wouldn't have had to come get me. They would have been sleeping peacefully in bed. My last words to my parents, were not words I wish to ever repeat. I thought I was so grown up.

I stumble into the bathroom before going to breakfast. I rub at the scar on the right side of my neck. My reminder every time I look in the mirror. The piece of the window that entered my neck, nearly killing me was shaped like a star of some kind.

I was told every day for years how lucky I was to be alive. I usually just smiled and said thank you. How lucky was I really? I got my parents killed and I was packing around a scar on my neck and a scar from wrist to elbow on my right arm to repair the bone damage. Damn I'm lucky. I think I might be a little bitter and sarcastic.

Nana would reprimand me every time she heard me say anything about it being my fault or unlucky to have lived. She has always been there since the accident. I started college shortly after the accident. I swore to become a nurse and help others as I had been helped. I have been out of school for a month now, working the night shift. I have always been a night person though.

I have a few days off work, so Nana decided to make me eat something since she says I'm getting too skinny. I remind her that I am athletically built, not skinny. She argues with me, but I need to be here to take care of her. She is failing more and more. There are times I think her mind is going. She starts talking about werewolves and Lycans as if they are real.

I would sit with Nana and listen to her stories, wondering where she came up with this stuff. She would talk about an alpha, the leader of the pack of wolves. A Luna was the wife of the alpha wolf. There was something she would talk about mates and bonds with mates. Maybe she was reading something. What was she watching when I wasn't there?

Nana decided that we needed to go for a drive today. She wanted to go see an old friend that wasn't doing so good. She said it would be a little bit of a drive. Nana usually drove herself, but she said she wanted me to come meet her friend while I still could. I agreed that on my days off, we would do more together, knowing her days were becoming more limited. After Nana was gone, I would have no more family. My parents had always been very private. I was sent to a boarding school far away. I was only home in the summers, not permitted to get far from them. So, no close friends here either. I usually felt like I was a dirty little secret with my parents.

I often wondered why my parents never had friends over or go out with anyone. I was never permitted to go stay with a friend overnight. I was always afraid that I was doing something wrong. My teenage years were very guarded. I was not permitted to go on any dates. My friends that I did talk to at school would ask if my parents were really religious or something. I never knew what to tell them. They weren't religious, just not trusting I suppose.

Chapter Two

It Starts : The Meeting

Nana wasn't joking when she said it would be a drive. We traveled for two hours before I started asking more questions. We had been traveling through the forest for more than an hour now. The roads were winding and small. I was enjoying the drive but didn't understand where we were headed to.

The fresh pine smell did wonders for my stress levels. I feel more at rest and comfortable in the forest. Nana told me that was part of my instincts. I would smile and shake my head at her weird comments. Can't help but to love nana.

"I'm serious dear. Your inner wolf is what makes you the strong athletic thing you are. You really need to talk to your wolf sometime. It would probably help you to feel better."

"Are you feeling okay Nana? You are talking kind of weird. You are talking about me having an inner wolf." I laughed as Nana just looked over at me like I was the crazy one.

"There are a great many things that we have never talked about, I think it might be time that we have that talk. Your parents made it very clear that we were never to talk about it unless necessary." She looked forward, lifting her head more. Like she was proud or something. "I think it may be necessary now."

"Nana, you are starting to scare the hell out of me now. What are you talking about?" I gripped the steering wheel tighter. I had pain shoot through my right arm with the grip. I winced in pain as I shook my right arm.

"Here's the turn." I applied the brakes as she pointed at a dirt road off to the right of the road. Nothing in sight besides a dirt road leading into the trees.

"We are out in the middle of nowhere Nana. The last town was about half an hour back. There is nothing up that road. You know we could get shot if we trespass around here."

"We are just fine dear, you will see."

"Nana, I think you may need to go into the doctor for a checkup. I am worried about you."

"Stop the car dear. I want to get out and stretch my legs for a minute. We have been cramped up for quite a while. This old body needs a stretch."

"Okay Nana." I shook my head in disbelief as she stepped out, holding onto the door stretching like she was warming up to run a marathon. I laughed at her as she walked around to the front of the car exaggerating her hobble. "You aren't that old." I laughed so hard that I snorted at her actions.

"You're right my dear." She stood erect, sighing. "There is that beautiful smile and laugh. You were hiding it from me. You see that tree line over there?" She pointed.

"Yes Nana, I see it."

"That is where my friend lives. You can't see it unless you open your mind though."

"What do you mean open my mind? Nana, did you take some medicine you weren't supposed to? Are you feeling okay?"

"I want you to do something for me. Close your eyes and vision that you are looking at a wolf." She looks at me with her face determined. "Just do it Nat. Do you think I would steer you wrong my dear?"

"Nana, we are making an appointment with the doctor when we get home. I will play along though if it makes you happy." I closed my eyes. I envisioned a great white wolf in front of me. The fur was as white as snow, eyes that flashed of a green. The wolf was larger than the average dog. The wolf looked at me as I looked at it.

I felt a pull or an urge to touch the wolf. I reached forward as the wolf stepped toward me. I kept my hand out as a sign of trust. The wolf sniffed my hand as it started to circle around me. I turned my head without moving my body, to watch it go around me. The white wolf stopped in front of me and sat on its haunches.

I stepped forward one more step, to actually have my fingertips brush the thick main of fur around its head. I sunk my hand into the silky fur. The white wolf whimpered at me as it lowered its head. I felt warmth and comfort rush through my veins. I heard the soft voice of a woman. I opened my eyes to end the vision I was creating. I looked around myself. No one was there but Nana sitting on the grass, soaking up the sun. The voice came to me again.

"Nana, did you hear the woman that is talking. I can't hear her words. Do you think your friend is calling out to you?"

"No dear. I haven't heard anything."

"Listen close." I closed my eyes again to focus on my hearing. The voice was clearer now. "My name is Kyra."

"There it was again Nana. Did you hear it?"

"No my dear. I can't hear your wolf. Only you can. What did she say to you?" She looked at me with a big grin on her face. Her green eyes sparkled in the sunshine.

"Now this is sounding crazy Nana. What do you mean, my wolf. The lady that spoke said her name was Kyra. I think we better get you out of the sun and back home."

"You are not crazy Natalie. I am your wolf Kyra." I jumped in surprise as the words and sound of her voice seemed to echo in my head.

"You didn't just hear that Nana?" I shook my head as I sat down with a thump next to Nana on the grass. Nana just shook her head no. I sat with my knees drawn up to my chest, arms over my knees while resting my forehead on them. I just needed to breathe.

"So your wolfs name is Kyra. That's a very pretty name. What does she look like? What did you see when you imagined a wolf? What color is she?" Nana sat there looking at me with such a serious look on her face. I started laughing like I was hysterical.

"Well, either you are not hearing me, or you are just ignoring me. Which is it? I really hope you don't think that you can just ignore me now after holding back for so many years. I couldn't talk to you until you were inside the lands of the pack. Guess what honey. I'm not going away now. Deal with me now or I may just drive you insane talking incessantly. Not to mention, we should really talk about the first transformation. You aren't going to like it much."

"Enough, enough. You are starting to give me a headache from all of the talking. I am now sharing my mind with a wolf?"

"I am not just any wolf. I am Kyra. Your wolf. The Goddess chose to bond us."

"I have officially lost mind now. Nana did you give us both some medication that we aren't supposed to take?"

"Look up the road dear. Do you see my friend's house now?" I lifted my head to look to the tree line. I could see not only her friend's house, but many houses.

"I am obviously hallucinating now. I didn't see those houses there before." Every scientific, logical thought just went right out the window. My head started to pound. Trying to think of any logic completely evaded me. "Nana, why are we here? Why are you just now telling me about this?"

"I received word that the Alpha of the pack was no longer here, I wanted you to meet your pack. Your mother was meant to be the Luna many years ago, but she suffered through a rejection from her mate, which might I say, is the best thing that could have happened. He was a terrible man. He was mean, ignorant, and didn't deserve her. He rejected your mother. She left the pack, met your father, and that's the short version."

"Maybe someday I will ask about the long version. I am still processing. All of these things you are talking about are just confusing to me, rejections, mates, alphas."

I had read a few romance books that talked about these things, but it was a few years ago. I thought that smut had been made up, someone's imagination in overtime. I guess it's just like any legend. You need something real to base the story from.

Chapter Three

The Pack /The Rejection

Nana and I both got into the car, heading up the road to the invisible homes. Well, until you go crazy, then you can see them. A large house stood in the center of the of all of the other homes. The large home had three levels to it. Glorious with a wraparound porch. A dream home for someone.

We approached wrought iron gates that opened as we pulled forward. A tall good-looking man pointed in the direction to our right. It seemed to be a parking area. I pulled up in silence, putting the car in park. I said nothing as Nana sat there with a smile on her face.

My car door was opened as I jumped with surprise. The tall man extended his hand to me to help me out of the car. I placed my hand in his, stepping out of the car. The man smiled at me, "I take it you are

Natalie?" I nodded my head in response without muttering a word.

Nana was out of the car, came over to me grasping my hand. I was pulled out of my trance that held me as I looked around in shock. "Well, you can be speechless. Didn't think it was possible." I looked around then realized the voice was from within myself. I shook my head, looking to Nana again.

Nana pulled me along with her toward the large house that I had thought was glorious. The closer we got the more glorious it became. We walked up the stairs to the large porch. The tall man held Nana's hand to assist her. He held open the heavy door for us to enter.

The inside of the house was just as glorious as the outside. The amount of carvings was breathtaking. A large office was just off of the open area. We were directed to the office. The door opened up to us by a large man with brown hair and blue eyes. Every inch of his body muscled and beautiful. "Hello ladies. I am Alpha Aaron Meyers. You must me the one they call Nana." He reaches out shaking her hand. "You must be Natalie." He reaches out for me to shake his hand.

A surge of energy jolts up my arm into my chest. I feel like I can't breathe. The weight of an elephant on my chest that let up as he let go of my hand. His eyes automatically went wide as he looked into my eyes. Kyra whimpered, let out a howl, talking about how he was our mate.

The alpha stood there looking at Natalie for a few more seconds before he walked around his desk again to sit in his office chair. He motioned for us to sit. Nana and I both took our chairs, looking at the beautiful man in front of us.

"This is Natalie as you know, I think it's time for her to get to know the pack. She has never been here before today. As a matter of fact, she met her wolf today, Kyra. I think I am approaching my end and we have no other family. I am hoping that the Waning Moon pack will open their arms, welcoming Nat." I watched Nana speak the words, but I really didn't hear much of what she said.

"I am currently in shock mode. I think my Nana took pills, maybe gave them to me, I have officially lost my mind and now I have talking going on in my head. I think I need to go outside for a few minutes. Please excuse me." I got up, running for the front door. My stomach knotted and heaved as I fought the bile rising in my throat. My mouth began to water as my stomach contents hit the ground just off of the steps of the wrap around porch.

I grabbed my stomach as I ran for the nearest set of trees I could see. My stomach contents once again heaved out of my body with a vengeance. My body racked with dry heaving as I stood there leaning against a tree. I felt a presence behind me. I was afraid to look as I was mortified that I had vomited all over the walkway. "I don't need anything thank you." I waved my hand behind myself.

"I thought maybe you could use a towel and some water." The smooth voice washed over me with a comfort. Why is that voice so familiar? I reach behind myself to grab the towel first then the bottle of water. I rinse my mouth then drank a few gulps. I used the towel to wipe my mouth as I turned to look at the person behind the voice.

Alpha Aaron stood a few steps behind me. "Thank you for that. I want to apologize for that. I'm so sorry. I will clean up the mess by the porch. I am so sorry."

"I actually came out here to talk to you about something else. I know that we are mates. I felt it too. I feel the draw to you, but I have promised my love to another. In your absence in my life, I didn't think I would ever find a mate. I was forced to take a chosen mate. I'm so sorry I have to do this to you." He dropped his head.

My mind raced with confusion at his words. None of this made sense to me. I have no idea what in the hell he is talking about. I have been heaving my guts out, now he is sputtering something to me that means nothing.

I, Alpha Aaron Meyers of Waning Moon pack reject you, Natalie as my mate and Luna." My chest hurt once again. As he spoke the words to me, Kyra was howling in a sound of pain. My heart felt like I was just stabbed, then it was taken out, stomped on, then splattered into a million droplets of liquid. "What the hell are you talking about? What is happening to me? Did you poison me or something?" My words had no effect on his facial expression.

Kyra howled again in agony. "He has just rejected us. That means, the Moon Goddess planned for you to be together forever, and he just told you that he doesn't want us. Is that clear enough for you?" I took a deep breath through the pain.

"I don't even know you. You arrogant asshole, can take your mate shit and shove it where the sun doesn't shine. I have more concerns in my life than dealing with a prick such as yourself. I don't need you. I never have. Now get the fuck away from me."

My body started to shake uncontrollably. I felt as if I was going to die. The loud howling of Kyra in my head caused me to lurch forward. I felt like there were knives in my body. The sensation of being ripped apart from the inside took over my body. I could feel and hear the breaking of my bones as my body changed. I had no control over what was happening to me.

Nana came out of the front door of the house as the process in my body started. She came down the steps quickly. In her hurry, she stumbled, she fell down the steps hitting her head on the walkway. She stopped moving as my body stopped ripping apart little by little.

Alpha Aaron ran over to Nana. My hearing was sharper. "What did you do to my girl? She is the best thing in the world. She only deserves the best." My sense of smell enhanced as I smell the putrid stench of the metallic blood mixed with the scent of Nana. I step forward realizing that I now have four paws, not two feet.

Kyra realizes what I am doing as she takes over the body of the wolf. My massive white wolf lunges forward toward the alpha. My teeth are exposed with a low growl emanating from my chest. He slides back with his hands up in the surrender position.

I stand over my grandmother. Her eyes are open, looking up into my green eyes. "I love you my baby girl. I will always be with you." I am screaming from within, but no sound leaves my now muzzle. I hear a howl coming from me. I nudge Nana with my snout, Kyra licks her face. Nana doesn't move. I nudge her with my snout again as my head falls back with the howl of death.

I turn again to look at the alpha. Kyra speaks to him through our mind. I am trying to accept all of this. I am so confused; I am crying that Nana is gone. "You are not my alpha. You have no control over us. You have rejected us. We will leave now but be warned. We are of alpha blood and royal Lycan blood. You have no idea what you just done to your pack."

"Natalie and I are not forgiving souls, Your promise of a fated mate was just betrayed." We jumped over the heads of all the people that had gathered around the scene. We ran off into the trees as everyone watched my departure.

Alpha Aaron and the rest of the pack stood there in awe as we disappeared as quickly as we arrived. Aaron lowered his head as his wolf Jax howls in pain. "You are an arrogant idiot Aaron. You just rejected our mate that is of alpha and royal blood. You will either find her and get her back or I will tear the world apart looking for her. She didn't finalize the rejection."

Aaron was beating himself up more than anyone would realize. He knew that Jax was serious about what he said. He was getting out of control without his mate. He had lied to her about another woman. He figured she was a weak human. She didn't even know about wolves until a little bit ago.

"Make sure to give her a proper burial. I don't want her wolf to return and know that her grandmother has been disgraced." Aaron hung his head as he walked back into the pack house. What had he just done? He rejected his mate, caused her grandmother to fall and die. He didn't want to think about what else could possibly happen.

Beta John went into the office with Aaron, shutting the door behind them. "What the hell happened out there? I saw the way you looked at her when they came in. Is she your mate? You have been waiting for her for a long time." He smiled sideways.

"I rejected her." Aaron spat out.

"Did you just say that you rejected her? Please clarify what I heard." John sat back in the chair with a huff.

"I rejected her. You heard me. I thought she was a frail, unworthy human. I lied to her and told her that I had a chosen mate. Her wolf obviously took over. That had to have been the first time she had shifted. She told me to beware, she was of alpha blood and royal Lycan blood."

"We all heard that Aaron. She had the link open for all to hear her words. Her wolf is the biggest I have ever seen. I'm sure she is bigger than you are. Not to mention, she is white. White is the rarest and most revered wolf color. She had a patch of fur on her neck that was red. It resembled a star."

In that exact moment Aaron had an epiphany. He knew that she was familiar to him. "I just realized that I really fucked things up."

"What was your first clue captain obvious?" John cringed as the alpha emitted a low growl while exuding his power as alpha. "Sorry. I didn't mean to offend you, but you really screwed the pooch on this." John chuckled softly to himself as the power hit him again.

"If you shut your damn mouth for a minute I will tell you why, besides the obvious." He sat again in his office chair. He spun the chair so that his back was to John.

"Remember the night of the accident, when my father died? My father had been drinking, reaching over to hit me as he plowed into the side of that car. The truck hit the car so hard that the car slid and a hit the trees on the side of the road."

"Aaron, why are you rehashing that accident? That was years ago. You stepped into the role of alpha then."

"Let me finish dammit. When I woke up I saw that my father was dead. I got out of the truck to go check on the people in the other car. I walked around to the passenger backdoor. When I looked in, a girl was sitting there. Her seatbelt firmly in place. Her arm was crushed between the door and her seat. She had a large piece of the glass from the window sticking out of the right side of her neck. She reached up for her neck. I grabbed her hand so she wouldn't touch the large piece of glass sticking out and make it worse."

Aaron turned to chair to be face to face with John again. "When I touched her hand I felt the mate bond with her. I stayed with her until the ambulance came to get her. She talked about how she was going to die. I thought she had died. I felt my heart shatter just after the ambulance pulled away. I felt her die. I went to the hospital after that. They wouldn't tell me anything because I was not family. I knew she was gone. I never told anyone about it. I didn't want to ever go through that pain again." He ran his hands through his hair.

"I didn't know for sure if I would get a second chance or not. I just know now that I am a coward. I never want to experience the pain of losing my mate again. I found her and lost her within a matter of minutes."

"Now the coward in me cringes. How do you tell your mate that your father killed her parents, didn't go looking for her, and now responsible for the death of the only family she had left in life? Tell me how." Both hands ran through his hair as his forehead came to rest in his palms.

"Send a search party to find her before Jax does something we all regret. He is shredding my insides."

Chapter Four

Solitude

We ran until my lungs burned, my legs made of lead, my heart pounding out of my chest. The fatigue took over my mind and body as Kyra found a small cave for us to rest in. I had no idea how far we had gone or where we were. My sense of smell told me that there were no other wolves around the area. I shut my eyes but for a mere moment as sleep took me.

He held my hand. Providing me the comfort I so desperately needed as I sat there whispering with death. The sounds became so faint. The smell of the blood in the car was so strong that it made me want to puke everywhere.

I was laying on a board now. The comfort was gone, the pain racked my body once again. I attempted to ask where the guy was, I needed him. I couldn't talk. For some reason they kept making my neck hurt?

Death continued to whisper to me as if a lover lay by my side. I listened closely as the whispers promised the end of the pain, the end of the torture. I see the lights flashing all around through the fog of my vision. I hear someone say that I had blood coming from my eyes.

The wailing of the sirens reminds me of movies I've watched. Well, that's weird to think about that right now. Where is that guy? I need him to help the pain go away. My body is shaking. I hear them saying that I'm going into shock from the blood loss.

I move my head to see where he went. I feel the pulse of wet and sticky on my neck. That's my heartbeat, that's my blood, how interesting. The shaking in my body stops. That feels so much better. Someone must have put me in a warm bath. I feel so light now. I must be on that cloud moving now.

I close my eyes for that warm hand reaching for me. Death whispers to me again. My body draws in the warm feeling that it gives me. I hear nothing but the whispers of comfort. I give myself to the whispers and promises. I'm ready to go now.

The sound of a snapping twig wakes me from my fitful sleep and nightmare. I move slowly as not to draw any attention to where I lay. Kyra sniffs the air cautiously. I am still in the wolf form. I guess I will be in this form until I figure out how to not be otherwise.

A squirrel scurries across the opening of the small cave. I stand vigilant at the cave opening, scanning the area. Kyra uses her enhanced hearing, sight, and sense of smell to determine if there is any danger. My body relaxes slightly as she sensed no danger close to us. I lay back in my spot to mourn the loss of Nana more. I can't believe that I had to leave her laying there like that. I hope I told her enough how much I loved her. I was responsible for another death of someone I love. If I had not lost my cool, leaving the house she wouldn't have come out to such a scene.

That pompous, arrogant, asshole had to make life suck just a little bit more than it did before. My future runs through my mind in a tangle of heartbreak. I have no family left in the world. I have no home to return to. Maybe I could go back to the house. What do I tell the authorities? My grandmother fell and died in a place that doesn't exist unless you are crazy, or a wolf like me.

I will be locked up in a nut hut for sure. I can't see any other future ahead of me now. I just started my career as a nurse. I will have to start an entire new life, new name, try to make some friends. I have no idea where to start with any of that.

The sound of wood breaking echoed through the cave again. I jump up to inspect the area again. The smell invades me of lavender and vanilla. I step back another step, head down, surveying the sounds.

A small voice wafts in on the breeze with the scent. "You can come out now. It's safe here. You are on common territory. No one will hurt you."

I poke my head out a bit farther to be able to look above the cave this time. The figure is dark with the sun setting behind them. It is a small, petite framed woman. My eyes focused to see that she had gray hair up in a bun. She had an apron full of tree limbs and other greenery.

Kyra stays on alert as I seem to be more trusting of the woman. I exit the cave completely to hustle behind a bush a few feet away from the woman. She approached me holding her hand out. I didn't sense any danger from her. I'm hoping it's not because she reminded me of Nana. Everything was so fresh in my heart and mind.

I take a step forward to sniff the woman more. She smiled so sweetly as I stepped forward. The pure smile with a twinkle in bright blue eyes convinced us that she was okay. She put her wrinkled and calloused hand into the fur on my head. I leaned into her touch out of instinct I suppose. Her smile never faded with the minutes that passed of her petting my head.

"You poor dear. What are you running from? Are you hurt at all? I don't see anything wrong. You are definitely a unique one dear. I have never seen a pure white wolf before. You are special. You obviously aren't a rogue." I lay at her feet as a whimper escapes me. "Come on my dear. You can come home with me. Let's get you taken care of."

The frustration built up within me as I was unable to say the words that I wanted to. The only way I could speak to anyone would be if Kyra spoke through our mind. This nice woman was definitely human. We would have no way to talk to her with any words.

We walked along the forest admiring the rays of sun that peeked through the treetops. The light breeze was warm and swirled the leaves. We approached a small log cabin that was easy to miss if you weren't looking for it. I could hear the sound of a river close by lightly trickling.

The woman opened the door, realizing I was actually too large to fit in the small cabin comfortably. "Dear why don't you shift back to your human form? You would definitely fit much better. Are you scared? Do you know how?" I whimpered and pushed my snout at her.

"This is your first shift, and you don't know how to shift back." I whimpered, nudging her hand again. "Okay dear. I understand. All you have to do is imagine yourself in your human form again. Focus on that. The wolf will step back, letting you forward again."

I focused on what I looked like in the mirror. I felt a chill come over me as my body contorted back to my human form. The bones rebreaking was not pleasant. I don't want to shift again anytime soon. I realize the chill is coming from me laying there naked in the ground.

The woman helps me stand as she wraps a blanket around me. The wool

blanket is itchy on my sensitive flesh.
"Thank you so much. I am Natalie. I don't
know if I would have ever been able to shift
back without your help."

"Think nothing of it dear, I am
Greta." She turns, opening the door for me
to enter. "That is much better." She giggles
slightly as she directs me over to the couch.
"You sit down and rest dear. Are you hurt?"

"Not physically, but mentally is a
whole other story." The tears that stung
behind my eyes trailed down my cheek. "I
just lost my grandma today. Sorry."

"You know, I came here to this place
as a lost soul too. Many, many years ago. I
decided to stay and hopefully help others to
find their path.

"You see many people come
through here, actually wolves, I should say."
Greta hands me a warm mug full of
something that resembles tea.

"Drink your tea my dear so you will
feel better. Nothing like a good cup of tea
to help you feel better." She sat in the
rocking chair next to the small fireplace. She
starts rocking as she mends on a chunk of
fabric. "So, you said your grandmother died.
What happened?" She never looked up
from her sewing material and continued
rocking.

My eyes welled up with the tears
that pooled with the thought of Nana. I
took another sip of the tea to keep the
tears at bay a little longer. "My Nana died
yesterday before I got here. It's a long story.
I miss her so much already. Nana used to
tell me stories about wolves and Lycans.
She was a great storyteller. At least I
thought they were just stories, until
yesterday." I closed my eyes as the well
overflowed. The tears crept down my
cheeks. I stared into the small fireplace to
focus my energies.

"I couldn't help but notice that you
have a few scars my dear. Where did you
acquire them?"

I pulled my attention back to the
question just asked. Less tears now from
that than Nana. "Several years ago, I was in
a car accident with my parents. They died in
the accident. I barely made it. I had my arm
crushed between the door and seat. Had to
have surgery done." I hold out my right
arm, bearing the scar from wrist to elbow.

"What about that star on your
neck?" Greta smiled sweetly at me.

"That's a scar from that accident
too. Some reason it has changed more and
more to look like a star." I took a deep
breath. "I had a piece of the window glass
go into my neck. I guess I was lucky to have

lived. I was told by the doctors that as soon as I was put into the ambulance that I actually died. They had to shock me several times to get my heart beating again. I guess that's why I decided to become a nurse. I have been considering continuing on to be a doctor myself." I took another drink of my tea.

Greta smiles, "done." Holding up the fabric she had been sewing on. "I have something for you to wear. It isn't much, but it will suffice for now. Go into my room and put it on."

I stand and reach out for the fabric. The fabric is much softer than the wool blanket rubbing on my skin now. I slide the gown over my head of a rich emerald green. The gown seems to change as I turn. I look down to see a satin gown with trim of gold. The sleeves cascade down my arms, the neckline plunges just enough to expose the tops of my breasts.

I tightly close my eyes as I truly believe I am losing my mind again. There was no way that the gown was changing. Maybe I was having some kind of a reaction or hallucination from the tea Greta gave me.

I walk out of the room to see Greta smile ear to ear. I look to her with confusion. "Just a bit of magic for you dear."

"Did you just say magic? What are you talking about? You are human, correct?"

"Well not completely. I am kind of like a witch you can say. I can perform some magic. That gown you wear will not rip or destroy with your shifting. You don't have to worry about being naked when you shift back to your human form. Let's just say, someone special gave me that fabric for you. I knew you were coming to me."

"What exactly did you put in that tea Greta?"

"Nothing except the herbs for the tea. I didn't drug you if that is what you are asking. You are not hallucinating. Now you lay down and rest my dear. We have much more to talk about after you rest."

The sound of the sirens diminished. The lights dimmed to dark as I grasped the warm hand

of death to take me. The pain and sorrow left my mind and body as I let the warmth consume me.

The light I approached was warm and welcoming. I closed my eyes once again to accept the warmth pumping through me. I felt a nudge as I opened my eyes to look upon the most beautiful woman I have ever seen. The tall slim woman had white hair that cascaded down her back to her waist. She wore the most beautiful light blue gown. Her eyes of silver sparkled with the light. The meadow we stood in was filled with wildflowers of all the colors of the rainbow.

The woman spoke to me without even opening her mouth. Her voice so soft and beautiful. "Natalie. You are destined for a very special fate. You are the key. You must go back and fulfill your destiny. You will know when the time comes." She turned, walking among the flowers.

I followed along beside her. I reached out to touch my fingertips to the flowers as we strolled together. "Why me? I am not special."

"Oh, but you are Natalie. You are a one of a kind. You are stronger than you realize. Someday you will see your path more clearly.

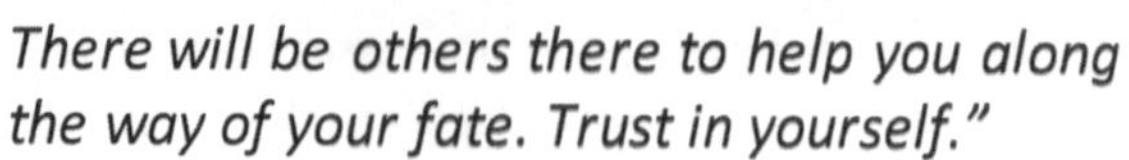

There will be others there to help you along the way of your fate. Trust in yourself."

We walked a bit longer. "What is your name," I asked her.

"My name is Celeste my dear. Someday your destiny will call to you, and you will remember this time we have spent together. Now go and fulfill your destiny."

She was gone instantly as I felt another jolt of energy run through my body. My veins were on fire as I opened my eyes to see people looking down upon me. "We have her back." The words echoed in my head. The pain and exhaustion took over my body and thoughts. I want to sleep now.

I awoke in the small bed in the bedroom. I was in Greta's room. How did I get here? That was the first time I had dreamed of that. The dream was not a nightmare. It was simply a dream. I had not been able to sleep without having the nightmare for quite a while now. This dream was different. I had never had a dream about a Celeste before. I know I had heard the name before, I just couldn't remember how.

Greta was not in the small cabin. I opened the door to outside to find her. There were some men there, talking to Greta. The asshole alpha Aaron was among them. He quickly turned his head my direction. I quietly ducked my head back into the cabin, quietly attempting to shut the door. "Natalie, you can come out now." Greta's voice was soft and calm. There was obviously no danger.

I knew I wasn't afraid of them. I just didn't want to see them. I had no reason.

Chapter Five

Return to the Pack

I was hesitant to leave the little log cabin for a few moments. I really do not want to face alpha Aaron again. He saw me heave my guts out, then threw me to the curb like I was trash. Not to mention, he got my Nana killed. My anger built up in me as I straightened my back and determination to leave the cabin.

I opened the door slowly. I stepped through the opening, closing the door behind me. I turned to the group of people to have all of them staring at me. I walked slowly with my head held high until I stood next to Greta.

"You will kneel to your Luna." I heard the authority come from Aaron to the other men present. The men all knelt in unison. Aaron included. I looked around to see who he was talking about. I would not kneel to another woman among us. Greta and I were the only other people around.

I looked to Greta in confusion. I heard her talk to me even though she spoke no words. "They are kneeling to you Natalie. You are the chosen mate to the alpha. Even though he rejected you, you did not finalize the rejection. He is here to talk to you. They have been looking for you. The alpha's wolf is how they found you. Do not fear his wolf. He will not harm you."

"I do not fear them Greta. I just want nothing to do with Aaron. He threw us away. He doesn't deserve the time of day. I don't need him." I turned and walked away from the group as all of the men stood, looking to each other in confusion.

I scanned my thoughts for all of the stories that Nana had ever told me. I remembered her talking about the Luna. She was the wife of the leader of the pack, the alpha. I am not his wife so that does not apply to me. I heard Kyra whimper as we walked to the riverbank. "What is wrong with you now Kyra? Why do you whimper like that? That is quite irritating."

"No matter if you don't want the alpha I still feel the mate bond that we have with him. I want us to go to him, but I understand the reluctance you have. I have it too." She continued to whimper in pain inside of me. I actually felt sorry for her.

I guess after all of these years I had just gotten better at hiding my feelings than most. My self-hatred has built a wall tall enough to compete with the great wall of China. I could completely block all of my emotions, or anything getting to them. I would probably be considered a cold-hearted bitch. It didn't bother me though. I did what I must to survive. My guilt had contemplated taking my own life multiple times. Nothing got through to my feel bads. I chuckled at my analogy of my feelings.

"Do you find something amusing Natalie?" The silky voice rolled over me in waves as I turned sharply to see Aaron not far behind me. "I have come to ask you to return to the Waning Moon pack. I beg for your forgiveness of my stupidity."

"I find it amusing that you have come all of this way to be told to fuck off. That is quite funny if you think about it." I snapped back away from Aaron as I swept past him to return to the cabin. He reached out to grab my arm. I saw red as I looked into his eyes. "Don't you ever touch me again!" I yelled so loud that the other men came running forward. I hit his hand away from me with such force that his arm came down to hit his own leg.

Anger rolled over Aaron as his wolf Jax took over. His body fell forward as the hair started to protrude all over his body, the snapping of the bones with moans coming from him. I stood there watching. Some of my lack of movement came to interest in watching, lack of fear, and anger beyond anything else I had ever felt. I kept Kyra at bay as I told her if I needed her I would let her come forward. I decided that with the reluctance, remembering the pain involved.

I stood in front of a snarling wolf. Staring at me with his bright blue eyes. Focused on me. I heard someone in the background comment that they needed to protect me; otherwise he would kill me now.

I took a step forward, probably out of stupidity and pride more than anything else. I pointed my finger directly at the wolf. "If you think you can come in here and scare me into coming back with you then you are sorely mistaken. You do not scare me. If you decide to kill me then go ahead and finish me off. I will not deal with anymore of this stupidity. I'm done!" I was screaming like a banshee as I watched the large black wolf in front of me lay down on his stomach then turn onto his side.

I didn't even realize what he had done until I stopped screaming and thought about it. The large black wolf with the blue eyes whimpered at me in submission.

"Kyra, what does this mean? Please talk to me. I need help here."

Kyra whimpered then let out the only way to put it, a purr. "He is submitting to us. He wants you to touch him. He will not hurt us. His wolf craves to have the mate bond. I have never heard of an alpha wolf submitting to a female prior to bonding. He is truly, seriously, utterly, submitting to us."

I hear the breaking of a limb behind me as I turn around to see all of the men standing behind me in wolf form. I look to the cabin to make sure that Greta is still safe. She is smiling ear to ear. I thought about asking her if she would like some popcorn to go with the show.

"You are different from Aaron yet part of him. Is that correct?" I look back to the large black wolf.

"Yes my Luna. I am Jax. I have waited for you for an eternity it seems."

"I am only Luna if Aaron and I are married? Does my memory serve me correct?"

"Yes Natalie. I would never allow another woman to take your place. You are meant to be mine, as I am yours. Will you touch me please Natalie. I want to feel your touch please. You will understand when you touch me."

"That is a rather odd request." I step forward to touch the top of his head, similar to when I met Kyra. I touch the main surrounding the head of the large black wolf. He emits a groan that vibrates his entire body. I feel the pulse run the length of my arm to the rest of my body as if it ran in my blood. I close my eyes to the feeling that takes over my body. I place both hands in his main to hear the vibration thicken into more with pulsing warmth through my body.

I savored in the warm contentment we were feeling until I heard the voice of Aaron whisper my name. I jerked my hands back at the memory that Aaron is in there too. "Aaron told me that he had a chosen mate now when he rejected me."

"He does not have a chosen mate Natalie. He lied to you for reasons that I will not attempt to validate to you. He must talk with you about that. I can guarantee that you are the only woman that will ever be the Luna of my pack. I know we have only met, but I would do anything for you, you are everything to me."

Jax bowed down to me, one paw out with his head down. I heard the other men behind me moving. I turned to see the other wolves bowing to me again. I turned back to Jax for him to stand and rub along my body. I reached out to run my hands along his body. A groan rolled out of his body.

"You are my queen Natalie. I want to claim you with every part of my being. I will control myself at this time if you come back to the pack with us. Please don't make me force you. We are meant to be together. I ask for a chance to win you."

"Jax, first of all I don't think you could force me into anything, but…. I will return to the pack at this time. I will make a deal with you though. If I choose to leave at any time you must let me leave. Do we have a deal?" I watched his eyes closely as he finally groaned. "I agree to your terms my queen." Jax ran his tongue along my neck as a shiver ran down my spine. His tongue so soft and warm, it surprised me. I felt his canine teeth graze across my flesh with a white-hot feeling as his tooth slid over my scar.

My body reacted to the sensations as my body lurched forward. The familiar sensation of my hair prickling, stretching, and bones breaking as I shifted into Kyra. As the shift completed I shook my body to adjust again to the feeling.

Jax and the other men knelt to me again as the white wolf that was larger than them stood there. I heard a groan emit from the chest of Jax as he circled my wolf, rubbing on her. Kyra purred with delight as I snapped her out of it. "We are ready to leave now."

"Greta, thank you for everything. Please stay well. I hope to see you again soon."

"You take care my dear. Remember all that we talked about, don't forget your dream. Follow your instincts. They will serve you well."

"Okay Jax, lead the way back." I followed behind Jax as we all ran toward home. The pace was much less rushed than the pace I carried to get here. It would take us two days to get back home.

We ran for the rest of the day, stopping to rest at the boundary of the pack property. My body was exhausted as I curl up in my wolf form for some rest. I felt safe with the other wolves around. I awoke during the night to find Jax curled up to me. I thought about objecting and moving but chose to stay warm and comfortable for now.

I woke to the sound of some of the other wolves moving about. Jax was no longer curled up to me. I stretched, moving my muscles that were slightly stiff. The process of shifting made me sore. I was definitely better than the first time I shifted though. My wolf body lay stretched out as Jax rubbed his muzzle on mine. This tongue came out to lick me as I pulled away from him. He grumbled with disapproval.

I couldn't afford to let even one brick crumble from my walls. One brick tumbling could cause a chain reaction. Jax had already gotten under my skin or fur as you could say, a little.

I could smell and hear the trickling of water not far from camp. I needed to drink more water. I was parched from the day of running. I approached the area carefully as I drank the water greedily. I could feel the presence of Jax behind me. "What is it Jax?"

"I am just protecting my queen. I found you and now you aren't going to leave my sight. I can't afford to lose you again. It would kill me."

"Did you just say again? What are you talking about?" I eyed him suspiciously.

"Aaron must spend some time talking with you. We will be at the pack house in a couple of hours. You will be staying in the pack house with us. I refuse to have you away from me."

"Wait a second. If you think you are automatically going to be climbing into a bed with me, you are dead wrong. No man will take advantage of me or force me to sleep in a bed with him."

"My queen, I apologize. You will never be forced into anything. I meant in the same house with us. I guarantee you will never get hurt by anyone, even myself."

"I just want to make sure that we are clear on that." I turned and walked back to the camp with Jax following behind me. He walked with pride as every wolf admired me as I passed by them.

It was time to get moving to finish the journey back to the pack house. We moved slower today as my muscles were more than happy to accept the reprieve from moving at a run.

I had been able to appreciate the feel of the wind rushing through my fur. The feel of my fur moving was like a tickle to my skin under it. The agility I had to move about was astonishing. I attributed some of the agility to my athletic build. I made sure to keep my body in shape.

Jax throws his head back and howls. It was a different tone as all the other wolves do the same thing. That must be letting the others know that it is us approaching. The howl is returned. We pick up the pace as we break through the tree line to the opening of the pack area.

We approach the pack house as several women and men exit the house with clothing for each person. I have a woman approach me as I will myself into my human form. The shift happens faster with less pain. I am still wearing my dress that Greta had made me. Looks of shock rolled over the faces of the other pack members.

I stood in place like a statue as the others were greeted by family and friends. I was frozen looking at the spot that I had left my grandmother lying when I ran away. I was so focused on my thoughts that I didn't hear Aaron talking to me. He placed his hand on my shoulder as I turned suddenly, grabbing his arm, stepping under, rotating his body to land on his back.

I stood over him holding his arm rotated as I had my arm drawn back with a fist. "Natalie, its only me. I wasn't going to hurt you. I was talking to you, and you didn't hear me."

I blinked several times as he talked to me, explaining. "I told you to never touch me again, didn't I?!" I yelled at him. I felt tears start to well up in my burning eyes.

"Show me where I will be staying." I demanded without delay as I walked into the pack house. Beta John was behind me in a matter of mere seconds.

I blindly walked toward the grand staircase. Beta John walked up next to me, motioning up the stairs. We got to the third floor as he turned left. "This is the guest bedroom for visiting extinguished guests. It will now be your quarters. The other bedroom on this floor is that of alpha Aaron. I am the beta, John. If you need anything, please don't hesitate to reach out to me." He opened the door for me to enter.

I entered the room, turned to John, "thank you. Please make sure I am not disturbed."

"As you wish Natalie." John turned on his heel skipping down the steps. I wonder why in the hell he's so happy? I closed the door leaning my back against it. I sank down the door with my hands covering my face as the tears took over. The sting of the tears caused Kyra to whimper for my pain.

Chapter Six

The Adjustment

I finally had cried until I had no tears left to cry. I decided to take a hot shower. I had not had one in several days now. I walked into the bathroom that made the Ritz look cheesy. I stripped down stepping under the hot water. The water ran down my back as I rested my forehead on the wall.

I let my mind wander to the times I wondered if I would ever find love. I had a few relationships but nothing more than kissing, holding hands. I never let a man close enough to love me. I am unworthy of being loved. I convinced myself of that years ago. The only worth I felt was being a nurse and returning the favor to those who saved my life years ago.

I was so focused on my thoughts that I didn't even hear the bathroom door open. A pulse of energy washed over me. A gasp escaped my mouth as my core tightened. My body felt as if fire ran through my veins. The blood rushed to my cheeks with heat. What the hell was going on with my body?

I turn around with the feel of a pull. Standing in the doorway is Aaron staring at me, naked and flushed. I am not ashamed of my body as I step out of the shower, in full view of his eyes. "Are you going to hand me my towel or just stare at me?"

"Just stare at you." He shakes his head, snapping himself back to reality, handing me a towel off the rack. I wrap the towel around myself as he turns away from me. "I knocked and you didn't answer. I came to check and see if you would like to eat. I was worried something was wrong. I heard your words of being unworthy of love."

"How in the hell did you hear my thoughts?" I stepped closer to him. He turned, looking into my eyes.

"We are mates. I can hear your thoughts if I focus on you." His voice soft and smooth.

"First of all. We are not mates. You made sure to break my connection to you with your rejection. Did you forget that already? You lied to me because I guess you just decided you didn't want me. You may still have a bond to me, but I don't have one to you."

"You gave up the right to call me your mate. I will come down after I get dressed for dinner. After that we are going to talk. I need to figure out how to, "accept your rejection" is what I was told, to finalize things. After that I will be going home."

Aaron lowered his head even farther before he left the room. He didn't know what to say to her. She was the most beautiful, fiercest creature he had ever laid his eyes on. Jax was whining the entire time she spoke. Since when does his wolf ever whine?

Aaron stormed down the stairs, went into his office with the walls shaking from the slamming of the door. John figured he better go calm the beast before they all paid the price for his stupidity. He couldn't deny the fact that the woman was fierce, beautiful and had a set of balls the way she talked to Aaron.

John entered the office after a quick knock. Aaron sat in his chair looking at the wall. "What happened?" John asked softly as to not feel the wrath.

"She is the most beautiful, fiercest creature I have ever met. Her tongue is sharper than a sword, slicing me into pieces in an instant. Not to mention the fact that Jax was whining the entire time she was slicing me up. She is right that I severed her connection to me. She intends on figuring out how to finalize the rejection so she can go home."

"Jax has been whining the entire time?" John asked with confusion on his face.

"Is that what you just got out of that? You didn't hear anything else? How can I be an alpha when all my wolf does is whine over our mate?" He turned to face John. He looked and felt like he had been dragged through hell. He needed a shower, to shave and get some sleep.

"I think that tonight you should probably avoid having to talk to her. If she completes the rejection Jax will unleash holy hell on earth. I will talk with her some tonight and try to keep her calm. You go to your room and get cleaned up and pull your head on straight." John shook his head as he looked at Aaron. Jax emitted a low growl at the thought of another man being around Natalie.

"You better hope it works. Otherwise heaven and hell will feel the wrath of Jax losing his mate again. I would suggest you don't touch her. If you leave your smell on her, I can't guarantee your safety."

John got up and left the office as he saw Natalie out of the corner of his eye. Aaron felt his heart break a little more as the scent of Natalie drifted into the room. The smell of the lavender and blueberries tickled his nose. Jax howled loudly for him to go to her. "I WILL NOT LOSE MY MATE AGAIN!" The words echoed in his head as a warning.

I met John at the bottom of the staircase. "Hello again Natalie. Good to see you. We have supper ready. When was the last time you actually ate anything? You must be starving." He extended his hand to me as I placed my hand in his.

We walked into the family dining room with a giant table. The décor looked antique but homey as well. It reminds me of Nana's home. John pulled a chair out for me to sit. I nodded at him for his politeness. He sat next to me and smiled. "Are you always in such a good mood? Sorry. I don't mean to be a bitch. Lots has happened in the last week now. I am still processing."

"No need to apologize Natalie. I understand you are going through too much right now. Maybe tomorrow we can just hang out while I show you around the pack. No stress, just a friendly chat and a friend to talk to."

I plump older woman carried out plates of food. The smells of the food made my stomach growl with hunger. I suppose I haven't eaten much of anything recently. I almost forgot my manners as I dug into all of the delicious food. As a nurse working night shift, you learned to eat fast or some nights you didn't eat. John laughed at me as I told him I was sorry. His laugh put me more at ease.

John talked almost non-stop the entire time. I felt he really was trying to connect with me some. He never asked me anything personal. I was grateful for that. He made sure to let me know that the walk-in closet in my room was filled with clothes for me per Aaron's order.

Whenever he would mention Aaron I would feel my body tense some. The man looked like he walked off of the cover of GQ with a rugged twist. His brown hair was short on the sides with it longer on the top, curved down just right to his eyebrows that framed his sapphire blue eyes.

I stopped for a moment, shaking my head of the thoughts of the man that I hated right now. How could he still be so damn hot? If it hadn't been for his rejection I would probably be jumping him right now.

John and I both jumped as we heard a roar or growl of some kind from the hallway. It was so loud that I think the painting shook on the wall. John jumped up to run out into the hall to make sure that no one had been hurt. He saw Aaron going up the stairs two at a time. We knew then what the sound had been.

John returned to the table sitting down again. "What in the name of god was that noise?" I asked between bites.

"I have no idea. Everyone must be fine or else we would know." He went back to eating like nothing had happened, so I did the same. By the time we were done eating all of the food that had been set in front of us, I was at the point of miserable and knew most everything about John.

"So in the morning do you want to have the grand tour then?" John looked at me with puppy dog eyes. I actually laughed out loud at his facial expression.

"I would like for you to give me the tour, but I do have some unfinished business with Aaron. I need to get some answers. I'm still confused on some things." I got up from the table as John stood as well. "Thanks for being a friend to me tonight. I really did need that."

John extended his hand to me for a shake. I laughed as I wrapped my arms around him, giving him a big hug. I left the dining room to go up to my room for the night. The size of that bed in there would probably swallow me whole.

I got to my door as I heard another shut. The moonlight shined in my windows just right. The rays made the room look even more extraordinary. I got undressed, realizing I didn't have any underwear and decided to not be foraging around in the closet, so I climbed into the bed naked. The sheets were soft, the bed swallowed me into a cloud. I looked out to the stars as my eyelids grew more and more heavy. I let the darkness consume my mind into a fitful sleep.

Chapter Seven

Jax and Aaron

Aaron paced in his room as Jax was growling. He had heard the comment she made about jumping him now if he hadn't rejected her. He had felt the rage leave his body as his power surged. He went up to his room immediately so no one would see him in this state. He had heard her laugh at John. Her laugh was like music to his ears. Aaron had to calm Jax several times from going down and ripping John limb from limb. He knew he should be the one to make her laugh, not cry, or be angry.

Aaron decided to make sure that Natalie was sleeping. He couldn't hear her thoughts any longer. He opened the door as quietly as possible after listening for a minute. She lay in the bed curled in a ball, whimpering. She was having a bad dream.

Jax growled at him to go to her. He was confused on how to approach her without her anger destroying him.

Aaron sat on the floor next to her bed for several hours watching her sleep. When she would start to whimper he would put his hand very carefully on her arm to calm her mind. He studied her features in the moonlight, longing to touch her more. A strand of golden hair lay over her cheek. His better judgement was lost in the moment as he smoothed the piece of hair back. Her skin as smooth as satin. She let out a purr from his touch. The connection was not completely severed, she responds to his touch.

Aaron left the room, thinking. She didn't seem to mind Jax so much. Maybe his way to her heart was through his wolf. It was worth a shot and Jax was more than happy to do anything for her.

In the hallway in front of Natalie's door Aaron shifted to Jax. He reminded Jax to be very quiet. Move slowly. Jax pushed the door open then leaned against it just enough for it to latch. He walked up to the side of the bed watching Natalie. She had a look of agony on her face. Their heart broke for her. He made his way around the bed.

Jax moved like a whisper. He gracefully got up onto the bed, lying next to

Natalie just enough to be touching her. Aaron reminded Jax to not groan. He felt the pleasure creeping into his soul as she lay still, not grimacing any longer. She curled up into him instead. The pleasure of knowing they brought her comfort washed over them as contentment calmed them to the bones.

His mind and body decided that if the loss was to happen again, at least me may have some time with her for the memories. To have happiness could be worth the risk. He knew in that moment that his entire life now depended on keeping Natalie next to him, loving him. He would put everything on the line just to feel her love.

I moved through the large pack house. I graze past something that pulls at me. I stop to look at the painting on the wall. The painting of Celeste. I feel her words echo through my head once more. I usually dream

about the accident. I am not having a nightmare.

I smell the mint and sandalwood aroma. I follow the path to the source. I pad softly up the staircase. I feel an energy pulling me. I am standing in front of alpha Aaron's door. Why am I here? I open the door to see him standing by the window. He has just his pants on. No shirt to obstruct my view of his muscled back. The tattoos cover the upper half of his back.

I long to touch his skin, trace the tattoos. I approach quietly as he turns, his hair messed up slightly. The distinct outline and shimmer of a tear trails down his high cheekbone. I watch it trail down to his jaw before dropping to his muscular chest. My mind screams to go to him and trail that tear. He steps forward, wrapping his arms around me before I can think long enough to move.

I meld into his body. The muscles twitch that are in contact with my skin. I realize now that I am wrapped in his arms naked. I reach up to trace the trail of the tear. "I'm so sorry my queen. I didn't mean to hurt you. I want you more than anything in this world. I fear love just as much as you do."

His hand comes up to the side of my face to follow over my jawline. He lowers his head, slanting his mouth to meet mine in a gentle kiss. A brush of soft lips that makes me want more. I lean more into the kiss and his tongue traces my bottom lip, so soft and wet. I want all of him as I open my mouth for his tongue to discover me. His hand starts at the base of my head to blaze a trail down my spine, slowly, torturing my nerve endings.

His hands reach my bottom as he picks me up, wrapping my legs around his waist. I snake my arms around his neck as I crave more of his touch. He lays me gently on the bed to place his weight over me. I squirm under his weight with the pulsing of my body. My core pulls for him to be a part of me. "You will be my first and my last." I hear myself say.

He whispers in a husky smooth voice next to my ear. "You are mine."

I wake up to the movement next to me. I open my eyes to see the black fur of Jax. I am curled up into his chest and stomach area. At first I panic not knowing what to do. Why is he in my bed? Is he the reason for the dream? I guess I still feel the connection some. I won't admit that to him though. I reach my hand up to lightly touch the fur next to my skin. I feel the groan escape his chest.

I revel in the feel of contentment and safety. I push my fingers into his silky fur even more. I close my eyes again, giving into the feelings. He is sleeping, he will never know how I am laying with him, admiring the sense of love and protectiveness I feel emanating from him. I push my face further into his chest to inhale the scent of mint and sandalwood.

I will lay here for a while longer to enjoy this before I get up. I close my eyes again. Jax opens his eyes but refuses to move. He keeps his breathing the same, so she won't know he is awake enjoying her attention. His heart raced faster. He was hoping that wouldn't give him away. He just needed this time with her. He needs everything about her.

The morning light forces me to open my eyes as I realize I am in the bed alone now. The emptiness made my stomach twist in knots. Maybe I will see how today goes. The thought of leaving here, Jax, and even Aaron made my stomach flop more. Why can't I fight this?

I decided I was going to prove something to myself. I got out of the bed, put my dress on, headed to Aaron's room. His door was shut but that didn't matter. I entered his room to him standing in front of his window. Just like in my dream. This time though he turned around quickly, looking at me in surprise or shock, maybe even fear.

I walk up to him, looking down at me as I tiptoe placing a hand on either side of his face. I placed my lips on his to see if there was any effect. I pulled back as he continued to stare at me. I felt my chest tighten and my core tingling. Maybe there was some kind of effect. I turn to walk out of the room.

Aaron grabs my arm, turning to face him again as he crushes his lips to mine. His hands firmly holding my head. I place my hands over his. I open my mouth to object as he invades my mouth with his tongue. I feel my resistance fade as I return his kiss. My body becomes putty as he wraps an arm around my waist to support me. His other hand fists into my hair.

The fire of my desire for him blazed through my body. Reality hit me like ton of bricks as I pull back. I back up enough that I am out of his reach. His eyes dark with desire search mine for answers. I have no answers to give to him, so I do what I do best. I ran. I went out of the room, down the stairs, and out the front door. A garden of flowers is dead ahead. My destination for the time.

Aaron was left standing there with more questions than answers. "Did that really just happen? Did I do something wrong?" They had made sure to get out of the bed before she awoke again to change her mind about us in her bed. We made strides with her last night and didn't want to ruin it all. Jax was left panting just as much as Aaron was. "I guess we let things happen at her pace. Maybe she will come to us again."

The smile faded from his face as the grim reality set in that they would need to sit and talk with her sometime, soon. He would need to face his fears as well. If keeping her came down to swallowing his pride and groveling to her, it would happen.

Chapter Eight

Explanations

I sat on the grass at the edge of the flower garden thinking. The problem is that I usually, okay, always overthink things. It's the nurse in me to always be thinking and observing. Evaluating, that is why I now sit here confused and wanting him even more than I did before. I realize all too late that I am sitting there thinking out loud. Bad problem I have.

Aaron is standing behind me. "You really need to make more noise when you approach people." I snapped like I usually do with him. His smile turns to a frown. I notice the twitch in his jaw as my eyes are evaluating every inch of his face. "Do you always piss people off, or is it just me?" His twitch returns to his jaw. My words affect him more than I guessed they would.

"I really think it is time that we talk some. Would you like to go to my office or take a walk?" The smile returns to his face. I straighten my back more as I tilt my head to think about my options. If I am in his office, I am trapped. If we are outside I can do what I do best if I need to. Run.

"I prefer to walk and talk." I bite my lower lip as my gaze drops to his mouth. My damn body is out of control. This really needs to stop. My mind keeps going back to the kiss.

"Come with me." He grabs my hand, lacing our fingers together, nearly dragging me. People all around stop and watch as we head for the tree line. I am almost stumbling along behind him as I pull my hand free.

"What the hell is your problem? You were just kissing me not that long ago and now you are dragging me to an unknown destination." I stop in my tracks, looking at his back.

Aaron turns around, within two steps he is standing within inches of our bodies touching. His muscled chest is heaving as I feel my heartbeat go double time. "You want to hear why I rejected you." It was more of a statement than a question. "I have loved you forever. I felt you die. I lost everything of my heart and soul in that moment. You show up and I turned into a coward. That is why I rejected you. I never want to feel that pain again. It scares me to death. You scare me to death."

I stood like a statue with my mouth open, like the words were just going to fall out that needed to. He grabs my hand again as he starts walking, without dragging me this time. We walk in silence until we enter into the trees. The soft warm breeze lifted some of my hair to cover my face for a moment as I run into the wall of muscle that had stopped in front of me. I had more questions now than I did before.

My brain raced around in my head at mach four on fire. What did he mean by died? Did his first mate die? Loved me forever?

Aaron leans over, whispering into my ear. "Don't move. Help is on the way." Grabbing my hand as a pulse moves through my body.

I closed my eyes tight as the memories flood my brain, eyes, ears, body, and mouth. I can see the blue eyes through a cloud of blood. I hear the voice and the sirens. I feel the comfort of him holding my hand. I smell the metallic blood, that dripped and pulsed from my body.

Aaron leans down placing his mouth over the star scar on my neck. I feel the warmth as the horrific parts of the memories leave my mind abruptly. "It was you. You were the one there after the accident." I opened my eyes to him standing up, looking into mine.

"I was not just there after the accident. I was in the other vehicle. My drunk dad was driving the truck that hit you guys." A tear made a path down his cheek.

I looked away as the reality was sinking into my hard head. I see a log to sit on. I feel the ground start to move beneath my feet as the trees sway in my vision. I sit with a hard thump onto the log. Aaron drops to his knees directly in front of me.

"We both felt the mate bond when I grabbed your hand that night. I tried to comfort you as much as I could. I didn't know what else to do. After the ambulance left with you, I felt you die." He dropped his head.

"My father died in the accident, just like your parents did. I became alpha immediately. I went to the hospital to find out more about you, but they wouldn't tell me anything. Part of me died that day as well." More tears fell from his eyes.

"After I rejected you, because I didn't want to ever face the pain of losing a mate again, I ended up realizing who you

were. You are my true mate that I thought
had been taken from me."

"I think I was also angry in a way. My
thought process went the wrong direction. I
figured if you knew I was your mate, why
didn't you come back to me? Why had you
left me alone for all of those years? Was it
to torture me for the evils of my father?"
He ran his hand through his hair. "I know
now that you didn't have any idea that you
were a wolf. You had no idea that what you
felt was the mate bond with me that night."

"I am willing to spend the rest of my
life making up everything, anything to you
that you feel is needed. I have thought
about you every day since that night." He
stood up again, pacing back and forth in
front of me.

"I feel ashamed that I didn't know
who you were when you came here. After
years of only seeing you in flashes and in
the cloud of darkness, I didn't recognize you
immediately. The star on your neck is what
triggered my memory."

"I'm so sorry for the death of your
grandmother. I feel that is my responsibility
as well. That it was my fault." He stopped
pacing to look at me. I felt the pressure of
his stare on me. I looked up to lock eyes
with him.

"What happened to my grandmother was a freak accident, that you did not cause. I don't blame you now. I did at first, but I was bleeding pieces of my heart."

"Why did you come to my room this morning and kiss me?" He kept eye contact with me.

"I am just learning about and trying to accept that wolves exist. You had told me we were mates and there was a bond. I was testing myself. I was testing a theory of the bond. I told you that you had severed that bond on my end. I really did try to convince myself of that. I was trying to prove you wrong if I really must admit it to myself."

"What is the hypothesis of your theory?" He lowered to his knees in front of me. A finger went under my chin, forcing me to look at his beautiful face.

I looked into his eyes for a moment before attempting to look away. His hand went around my throat gently, forcing me to look in his eyes. "Tell me you don't want me. Tell me that you felt nothing during that kiss, and I will let you walk out of here." His tongue came out from between his lips to wet them. My throat was so dry. If I told him the truth, I was showing weakness, if I lied, I would lose him forever.

"I will make the question easier to answer. Did you feel something during that kiss? Yes or no."

It came down to one word. "Yes."

"That is all I needed to hear." His lips came down over mine with a heat that took my breath away. I struggled to make any sense of what was happening to me. He pulled me forward off of the log onto his lap. My arms went around his neck, as he held my head to deepen the kiss even more.

Aaron's eyes glazed over as an emergency call came out that one of the children in the pack had been hurt and needed help. The pack doctor had gone into the town for supplies. I heard the cry for help too. Aaron didn't realize that I could link with anybody. "I can help. I'm a nurse."

I sent the link back out to meet us at the doctor's office. We would be there as soon as possible. Aaron looked at me with confusion.

"There are lots of things about me that I am learning, and you don't know either." I smiled, jumping off his lap, extending a hand to him. We took off for the doctor's office.

Chapter Nine

Place in the Pack

"Where is the doctor's office?" Aaron grabs her hand, directing her to the office. As they get to the office there is a woman running toward them holding a small boy in her arms, crying. "He fell out of a tree while playing and now there is a branch through his leg."

Aaron sat the boy on the exam table for me as I talked to the mother on the way into the office. She was calm by the time we entered. I looked at the young boys leg while continuing to talk to the mother. "He has lost so much blood." The mother was starting to get worked up again.

The limb had gone through his thigh, protruding out the other side. He was losing more blood than just a couple of drops. I tied an ace bandage above the limb to slow the bleeding while I gathered the supplies to start an IV on him to increase his fluid volume again. The poor boy looked so pale and scared. My heart ached for him. "Aaron, we need to get him to a hospital."

"Natalie, we can't take him to a hospital. They would find out he is "different" than he should be. That is why we have a doctor here."

"Call the doctor and put him on the phone for me then."

Aaron had the phone out and the doctor on the other line as I got the IV started. "Put it on speaker phone."

"This is Doctor David Harris."

"Hello Doctor Davis, I am Natalie, and I am an emergency room nurse." I told him what was going on and how the boy was doing. I did as the doctor told me as he walked me through what to do. As I got the stick to the point of coming out of the skin it must have torn the artery open more. Not good, going to bleed out in a matter of a minute now. I grab the clamps as I have Aaron shine a light for me. I clamp both sides of the artery around the torn spot.

"You know I don't do stitching, but I had a doctor once that took to teaching me how to do sutures. I got the supplies as I started to sew his artery back together before he lost his leg in the process. I released the clamps after I hoped it sewn up good enough. No blood coming out. I had done it. I decided I could breathe again as I cleaned the rest of the wound.

The boy started to heal the second I had cleaned the wound. He is lucky he is a wolf, or he would have died I'm sure. The boy had lost so much blood that I was worried about complications. His pulse was present, but his heart had me worried.

All of a sudden I felt a surge from my chest and the words in my mind, "You are of alpha wolf and of royal Lycan blood. Your blood is the healing power. Use your instincts." I gasped as I returned to what I was doing.

"Are you okay Natalie? It's like you went somewhere else for a few seconds there. Your eyes glazed over like you were linked to somebody."

"I'm okay. I know what to do." To the horror of the mother and Aaron, I unwrapped the wound which still seeped as it healed. I grabbed a scalpel from the surgical tray, slicing the tip of my finger. I let my blood drip into the wound.

To all of our shock, we watched as the wound was healing before our very eyes and his heart function returned to normal again. The wound sealed with only a very thin scar.

The young boy sat up smiling. "Look Natalie, we have the same star on us now." As he pointed to my neck then his leg. I touched my scar to have an instant burning sensation. It was gone as it happened.

The mother of the boy threw her arms around my neck, praising thanks to me. The little boy looked up with his big brown eyes lovingly. "Thank you Natalie. I love you." He wrapped his arms around my legs then ran out the door with his mother hot on his tail.

"That poor woman has her hands full." I turn to clean up the area as Aaron wraps his arms around my waist from behind me. He moves my hair from my shoulder as he kisses my neck. "You do realize you just saved that boys life?"

"That's what I am trained to do, why I went to school." I smiled at his praise. For some reason it mattered from him.

"By the way, he lifts my hand, looking at my fingertip that was already healed. What was that all about?" He held my hand, rotating it looking at my finger with a grin after he kissed it.

"When you asked me if I was okay. I had a pulse of something and then someone telling me that my blood was the answer and follow my instincts. It was the weirdest thing."

"It is fate that you were here to save that little boy, and his scar matches yours. Ironic I would say." He smiled as he kissed my neck again. I was kind of getting used to this attention thing he was doing.

"Now, I would like to go take a shower and get cleaned up. I have blood all over me now. I think you need to get a shower too. Get the blood out of your clothes before it stains."

His mouth close to my ear, "would you like me to wash your back for you my queen?" I think I may have purred a little bit.

"I don't think this time thank you." I smiled sweetly up at him.

"Okay fine. You don't know what you are missing out on though." He gave me a sad look with a head tilt. The puppy dog eyes included.

"Get out of here." I giggle as I shove him toward the door. I really didn't know, but I sure as hell wasn't going to be telling him that. I guess letting someone that close to me had never been an option. I have walls to protect.

I received a few odd looks as I headed back to the pack house, blood covering the front of my body, but no one freaked out like I thought they would. This is a totally different world than my norm.

I step up on the first stair of the pack house to hearing my name called behind me. "Natalie, Natalie, will you show everyone else that we have matching stars?" A group of children came running up to me with eyes large and full of inquisitiveness.

"Okay." I push my hair to the side as the children oh and ah over my scar on my neck. "See, it's the same." All of the children start squealing and jumping around. Wrapping their arms around me as I watch with curiosity as to the purpose of the excitement of a scar, but I loved it. I returned the hugs as fast as I could, with them moving so quickly. All I could do was laugh at the happiness surrounding me. "No more getting hurt, okay? Now you go play nice." They all ran away screaming and yelling, "Bye Natalie, I love you."

I yell back to the crowd of children, "bye, love you too." I froze in place as I realized what just fell out my mouth. My Nana had been the only one to ever hear those words from me. I swear this place is turning me soft. Now off to the much-needed shower. I giggle as I ascend the staircase to my room.

My body felt like I had been ran over and dragged for a few miles with the adrenaline dump diminishing in my veins.

Shower then nap sounds good to me. I bundle my clothes, laying them on the countertop. The hot water washed over my body as I rinsed my hair.

I open my eyes to Aaron standing just outside of the shower, naked. "I invited myself in, sorry. I would like to reward you for what you did today." He backed me up to the cool tile on my back. I was too surprised and my body on fire, I couldn't turn my brain on to object.

I stand with my back on the tile wall as Aaron puts a hands on the wall, either side of my head. I can't seem to catch my breath as he leans his mouth down over the scar on my neck. His tongue darts out to roll over it. I gasp for a quick breathe as he whispers, "I need to taste all of you. I want to pleasure you." I feel my body shiver as his words caressed over my skin like a satin blanket to settle in my core.

He traces his tongue down my collarbone to my breast at which he doesn't stop. He runs his tongue over my hardened nipple to continue over my ribcage, only pausing to kiss occasionally. The path down my body was causing my blood to boil. I kept my hands plastered to the wall behind me, to keep me grounded.

His assault with his tongue continued to my stomach. The twitching of my muscles makes him groan with the pleasure of my response to him. His tongue circles my belly button as he goes lower. I was so consumed in the sensations I had not noticed the hand sliding up my leg. He reaches behind my knee, lifting my leg up and over his shoulder.

The warm water washes over my core as his tongue presses at my clit. I nearly jump out of my skin at the sensation. His tongue continues to stroke as I feel the tightness in my core building. The pressure becomes so intense that I feel my hips rocking to his motions. He applies more pressure to my clit as I feel his fingers entering me. I feel the explosion in my body as I scream with the pulsing of my entire body. I grab his shoulders to steady myself from falling. He stands up pinning my body to the wall with his. The muscles twitching in his chest as he slants his mouth over mine.

I taste myself on his lips as he takes all of my air from my lungs. My body continues to quiver with the heat of our bodies. I can feel his passion against my stomach. Hard and pressing into my flesh. He reaches over to shut the water off, running his hand down the side of my body. "Mine." I hear his low growl.

"I don't think I can walk," I finally find my words.

"You don't have to." His crooked smile made my heart skip a beat as he picked me up, cradling me to his chest. He sat me gently on the bench, handing me a towel. I couldn't help but to stare at his magnificent body. He was the definition of man. No textbook could compare to him. "Do you like what you see?" His voice just above a whisper.

Having seen more than my share of naked men as a nurse helped to keep me from being shy from the question. "Yes. Like nothing I have ever seen before." I think the maker had been more than generous with proportion.

As he looked away I stood, wrapping the towel around myself as quickly as possible. He had not looked at me again yet, so I took the opportunity to leave the bathroom to be able to breathe again. I took a deep breath as I entered the closet to get some clean clothes.

My body and brain remained in a state of shock. The remnants of the orgasm remained, lingering in my core. I craved more, but to let him closer would mean to let my walls down. I have learned my lesson well.

I walk out of the closest dressed again as Aaron sits on the chair in my room waiting for me to come out. He eyes me top to bottom. I start to feel the heat building within me again.

Chapter Ten

The Resistance

The intensity of his gaze made me fidget like a damn teenager with my hands behind my back. I was becoming very self-conscious. "Why are you looking at me like that?" I can't take the silent stare any longer.

"So, have you been under a rock since the first time we met?" He grinned with his comment.

"I lived with my grandmother, went to school minding my own business. I have not had time nor want for any type of relationships. Why does this concern you?" I stood a little taller. "I don't have to explain myself to you. Why do you care so much?"

Aaron stood from the chair stalking toward me like I was his prey. "Every man wants his mate to only know his touch, his smell, his desire for her. Feel only desire for him as well." He approached closer. I felt as if my clothes were being taken off of my body with each step and breath he took.

I continue to stand in place as if his words have no effect on me. I hold my breath so that he can't hear me gasp when he gets close enough for the smell of him to invade my better judgement or senses. If I can keep him far enough away from me, I will be okay. That little devil voice in my brain decides to speak up, "just keep telling yourself that, you're an idiot."

At this point I could have reached out, putting my hands on his chiseled chest. His eyes never broke contact with mine the entire time. I stepped back as he took another step toward me. We repeat the movement twice before my back comes into contact with the closet doors.

I held my arm up, my palm over his pounding heart. I took a small, long, drawn-out breath to avoid a gasp again. "I think we have things to be doing right now, places to be." I needed the madness to stop in my brain and body.

"We do have things to be doing right now. There is something I need to show you that I can do to your body. Something that you do to my body. You may have taken anatomy classes, but I don't think you can truly appreciate them yet." He puts his hands on either side of my head. The pressure he puts on my arm makes me move it down his body.

I hear a growl rumble in his chest as my hand moves down. I instinctively pull my hand away. "You don't need to take your hand off of me. I actually prefer your hand on my skin. You really have no idea what you do to me, do you?"

I turn my head with the warmth growing in my cheeks. I saw what I did to him, but that doesn't mean I am going to jump in bed with him. His mouth came down, not quite touching my neck, just below my ear. His breath was warm and sweet. I took a breath in holding it. "Let me demonstrate for you." He reaches down with his hand grabbing mine. He places my hand directly over the bulge in his partially undone jeans.

He pushes himself more into my hand, curling my fingers slightly around the length. "This is what you do to me." The words whispered on my neck sent a shiver down my spine. "You are mine. I will claim you, then I will mate with you. Making you beg me to claim you over and over." The points of his sharp teeth scrape along my sensitive skin.

I feel a rush of adrenaline as I realize he is about to bite me. Mark me. I duck down and shove under his other arm. I caught him completely off guard as I kick the back of his knees taking him to the floor. "I will not be claimed or mated as you put it. I am a human too. I will be treated with the respect that I deserve. I am not some dog in heat for you to play with." The shock of what I just did to the alpha of the pack rattled my brain.

I turn to leave the room as he quickly recovers, jumping up to catch my legs, bringing me down to the floor with a thump. His much larger body covers mine as he holds my arms above my head. His legs cover mine so that I can't move. I scream at the top of my lungs, probably more out of shear disappointment than anything else. Aaron places his mouth over mine. His lips soft and supple as he sucks my bottom lip in between his teeth.

My body betrays me once again as his heat consumes me, my mind melting. He releases my lip, placing another kiss on my lips. "I will not hurt you Natalie. You never need to fear me. I would rather slit my own wrists than to hurt you." He lowers his head more, letting out a breath.

"I don't know what I just did wrong. The things I said, I'm sorry. I didn't mean to disrespect you. I'm sorry. You win." He looked back up into my eyes as he once again kissed me passionately. He released my hands, stood up and left my room. I was confused. What did he mean by, "you win." Were we in some competition?

I got up off of the floor, heading into the bathroom to pull my hair up. My body ached with need from how close he had been to me, the way he pleasured me in the shower. I start to give in, and I swear to god I hear a brick fall, bringing me back to where my mind should be. My wall took years to build to perfection for some pretty boy to come along and destroy it, ripping my heart out along the way.

A knock came at the door just as I stepped out of the bathroom. "What is it now Aaron?" I opened the door to John standing there wide eyed looking at me. His hand still in the position to knock.

"I was coming to let you know that tonight a celebration is planned in honor or you. There will be food and celebrating on your behalf. Nothing formal. Wear whatever you are comfortable in." He looks at me as if he just spit that all out as fast as he could so that he could leave. I chuckled at the look on his face.

"I don't suppose you have seen Aaron for a while have you? I need to let him know what is going on tonight." He smiles broadly at me.

"I'm not sure where he is. He was here not that long ago. Can I ask you for a huge favor though?" I tucked my head and smiled coyly to him.

"Anything. I told you if you need anything to just let me know."

"Aaron made the comment to me that I won. Can you tell me what he was referring to or could you find out? Please? I'm just a little bit confused by that statement."

"I don't know for sure what he meant but I can find out for you." He scrunched his face like he was in pain.

"Thank you so much. I really appreciate you doing this for me." I wrapped my arms around John in a big hug. "My only friend that I have in the world right now."

"I will see you in an hour then. Just come out front. The party will be starting when you arrive."

John turned to walk away as he sees Aaron open his door, motioning for him. John just knew that Aaron and Jax were going to go nuts. He grimaced as he stepped into Aaron's room and was shoved against the door after it shut.

"Did you touch our mate? What the hell are you thinking?" Aaron inhaled deeply of Natalie's scent.

"I didn't touch her I promise. She gave me a hug and said I was her only friend." John held his hands up in surrender from the wrath that was Aaron and Jax.

Aaron let go of John's shirt, with him landing on his feet that had been off of the floor. "I don't know what I need to do to get through to that woman. She keeps trying to push me away, just as I think things are going well. I take one step forward to take two steps back it feels. She is driving me insane. Do I let her leave and just deal with the consequences?"

"Natalie asked me what you meant by saying, "you win." I told her I didn't know, but she is interested to know. I don't want to overstep my bounds here, but it seems like you may need a wingman for this one. She's tough."

"I told her that she wins at the trying
to push me away. I guess even if I can't
have her, as long as she is around, Jax will at
least not destroy the world as we know it."
He ran his hands through his hair in
frustration.

"Maybe she will warm up to you.
Just give her a little more time. I'm sure she
will change her mind about you and Jax. She
has had a lot thrown at her in a short time
man."

John grabbed the handle of the door
to leave as he turned to Aaron. "The sight of
that spitfire taking you down and reducing
Jax to a puppy is worth it's price in
admission alone." He flung the door open
and ran like his ass was on fire, laughing like
a madman the entire time. The mind-link
came a couple minutes later that the
celebration was to be held tonight in honor
of Natalie. Be there in half an hour.

Aaron thought hard about John's
words. Maybe she did need a little bit more
time, move a little slower with her. After all,
he was pretty sure that in the shower he
felt the evidence of virginity. The epiphany
hit him in the face again.

He decided that he was the dumbest
man on the face of the earth. She had never
been in love, and she was in fact still a
virgin. That is why she keeps pushing him

away. She is scared. She is scared of him and his love. His heart ached at the thought that she may fear him, but it wasn't from what he had done.

He decided that he was going to take his time to earn her love and not expect it. As long as he had her here he had the chance to work his way into her heart.

I walked outside of the pack house in a nice summer dress that I had found in the closet. My sandals complimented my outfit of choice when I didn't wear my tennies. Simple and to the point. My long blonde hair hung in a braid down the side. I have no idea what kind of a celebration they could be having for me, but I guess I will find out soon enough.

The hoard of children came running up to me again as I stepped out. Little arms reached for hugs. I received a kiss on the cheek from every one of them. I giggled the entire time as they hugged, kissed, and then ran off yelling they loved me. I looked for the little boy. We wasn't in the group. Looking around worried, I spot the little boy with his mother approaching me.

The little boy walked up to me with a bundle of flowers that he had to have picked himself. "I want to give these beautiful flowers to a beautiful Luna. Thank you Natalie."

I accepted the flowers as he wrapped his little arms around my neck. "What is your name little man?"

"I am Luke. This is my mommy." I chuckle at the response that mommy has no other name according to children. "I am Ana." His mother smiles, introducing herself.

I feel a warmth creep up my spine as I look behind me to see the gorgeous man leaning on the door frame smiling at us. He affects me without even trying. I can feel when he is near.

"Where is your daddy Luke?" I return my attention back to Luke and Ana.

"My daddy died. He watches over me though. I talk to him. I told him all about you. We both have the same star now and you made me all better." He didn't appear to be sad, but I watched the look of despair cross over Ana's face.

I am realizing there are so many things that I need to learn. I have been so wrapped up in myself to notice that I need answers to many questions. I need some direction in this new life.

Chapter Eleven

The Celebration

As Ana and Luke walk away, the rest of the pack members start to approach me to thank me for what I had done for Luke. They all referred to me as Luna. I didn't correct anyone. I really didn't know what to say to it. Aaron never left the spot that he hovered in.

The crowd started to direct me toward a set of tables that formed a long table. The tables were filled with all kinds of food. Everyone in the pack had brought something to share. I had never seen so much love among people than I did in this moment.

At the table I had my chair pulled out for me by Aaron, who then sat next to me at the table. The aroma of all of the different food made my stomach grumble with hunger. Aaron handed me a glass of wine as he stood to make a toast to me. "I would like to toast Natalie and her gifts that she brings to the pack. Your Luna is a remarkable woman." The cheers came from all as I looked to Aaron about his Luna comment.

The food was being passed around as all smiled, laughed, and had a great time together. Everyone watched me as the meal continued. I started to feel slightly conscientious after a while. Aaron leaned over to whisper in my ear. "You look amazing tonight." The tickle of his breath on my ear causes me to scrunch my shoulders and giggle. He grabbed my hand, placing a kiss on it.

I know I blushed as my face felt like I was looking into the fire that roared in a pit not far away. The flames danced to a slow provocative song. The only time these thoughts invade me is whenever Aaron is near me.

I attempted to distract myself from his presence. I needed to find something to talk about or leave and do. I decided to get some answers. If he is so eager to please me, he might actually sit and answer my questions.

"I have a few questions to ask you. I guess I don't know who to ask questions." I turned my body in my seat so he couldn't touch me as easily.

"What would you like me to answer for you? Anything." He smiled as he focused on me. I could tell he was trying to be nonchalant about looking at me too much.

"What happened to Luke's father?"

"I guess there is no beating around the bush with you." He laughed as he turned to me more. Now we were touching the entire time, not just occasionally. Damn he is good.

"Rogue's attacked our pack last year. We sustained many losses from that. His father died protecting our pack. He actually saved my life to be honest."

"So, you talk about mate's all the time. Do all wolves have mates chosen for them, or it just happens? I'm not all the familiar with this stuff."

"The Moon Goddess is the one who chooses the mates for each of us. Every wolf has a mate selected for them. Once your mate dies, it takes a strong person to survive the pain that comes with their death. Occasionally there are second chance mates. I actually thought at first when you arrived here that you were a second chance mate. I didn't want to go through the pain of losing another mate, hence the rejection." He bowed his head.

The look of pain on his face caused a pain in my chest.

I must have had a look of shock on my face as when he looked back at me, he gasped like something was wrong. "Are you okay? Is something wrong?"

"I am fine. Anyway, so mates are determined by the goddess and will sometimes give a second chance mate to some? How does she determine if someone is deserving of a second chance or not?"

"Wolves are social and need to have others around. That is why there are packs. The rogue wolf has usually been banned from a pack for a reason or so they choose to remain alone. They are still given a mate. Wolves don't do well alone. Look at me for example."

"You look like you are fine. What do you mean?"

"Jax has been getting slightly out of control without his mate with him. He is lonely and the mate is the one that soothes pain and thoughts. Wolves are very devoted to their mates. They are very attracted to them and find great pleasure in each other." Aaron gazed into my eyes with a twinkle. His side smile said a mouthful without moving his lips.

"I will show you what I mean. Think about something that makes you sad. Close your eyes and think about it for a second."

I close my eyes as I think about the loss of Nana. I feel the sting of tears behind eyes. Aaron brought a hand up to the side of my face. The pain of the memory changed to good memories with her. I opened my eyes to look at him.

"You were thinking about your grandmother. I could feel your pain. The mate bond brought you the comfort you needed." He removed his hand as I felt the sting of the tears return to me. I grabbed Aaron's hand. The pain once again stopped as I felt content.

I looked up into the smiling blue eyes. "What did you mean when you said that Jax was getting out of control?"

"Without you here with him, he is reckless, more daring, takes chances that he shouldn't. I guess you could say that he is on a self-destructive path without someone to love him. The only person that he would never hurt is his mate. Without that calming effect there is no control over the powerful wolf."

He continued to gaze at me. "So, I have a question for you then. Does Kyra want to have Jax around? Does she feel him too?"

I knew that was a fully loaded question. He was looking for me to admit that we still felt the connection to him.

The scream tore through the air as the link came that there were intruders approaching the packhouse. The instant reaction for the rogues to attack, all women and children ran for shelter as all that were warriors, protectors, remained for the attacking intruders.

Every one of the warriors had shifted into their wolf. I felt the need to help in any way I could. I didn't want any of these wonderful people to get harmed. I would help to protect them. I summoned Kyra as my shift started. The shift happened quickly without the pain. My senses were enhanced and ready for whatever I had to do.

My large white wolf stood at ready. The pack formed a circle around Aaron and I. The warriors would die to protect us. The first attack came from a large black wolf. He immediately killed one of the pack with precision. The other wolves emerged from the tree line on a dead run at us.

There were still women and children trying to get to safety as I watched a wolf lunge at Luke and Ana. I felt a rage unlike anything I had ever felt take control of my body. I sprang over the circle of wolves to head off the rogue from the pair.

I instantly drilled into the side of the wolf that flew farther than I would have thought. He got up, shook off his pain, lunging at me again. I was able to move out of the way of his attack. He persisted to come at me again. I was much larger, able to grab him by the throat that crunched grotesquely as I clamped my jaws.

The pack was fighting with the other wolves as I turned to return to the fight. I was hit from the side as I flew with such force that I hit the tree near me. I felt the sharp pain as a rib broke with the impact.

I heard a loud howl come from my right as I see Jax looking my direction from realizing my pain from the broken rib. His eyes flashed ferociously as he left the fight to attack and rip the throat out of the wolf that had attacked me. He licked my muzzle before we both turned to evaluate our attack.

I lunged at a wolf that was attacking another wolf from the pack. I heard the crunch of the bones in the throat of the wolf before I was jumped on by the large black wolf that had attacked first. He went directly for the star on my neck with fangs. Two other wolves jump onto my back as well. I am pinned down as I realize Kyra starts screaming.

"We need to get up. He is meaning to mark us. He is here to claim us." I struggled a few more seconds before Jax lunges at the wolves on my back to get them off of me.

The wolves went rolling off of my back as the large black wolf snarled at Jax then bounded off into the tree line. I grabbed one of the wolves by the throat before he could escape. I was much larger, and he begged for mercy from me. "Change back to your human form or I will snap your neck right now." I demanded with the mind-link.

The rest of the pack had gathered around as they all shifted back to human form. I was surrounded by a bunch of naked men, with my jaws wrapped around a man's throat.

Aaron was the first to be by my side. "Why did you attack our pack? Who is your alpha?"

The man struggled to breathe as I loosened my grip on his throat, so he could talk. "We don't care about you dumb wolves. We are here for her."

"Who is her?" Aaron knew but needed the clarification.

"The bitch that has me by the throat." I applied a little more pressure to make him choke and gasp for air. The gurgling of him attempting to breathe brought me some kind of satisfaction.

"Kyra, I need more answers please." Aaron put a hand into my main to calm me.

"Why did you come for her? What do you want with her?" The look on Aaron's face screamed the rage he felt with the attempt on me.

"She is the fated hybrid with the gift of her blood. She is of age, unmarked and unclaimed, leaving her open for another alpha male to claim and mate. You know the laws. Even if the alpha is a rogue." I felt the rage boil up in me again as I heard those damn words of claim and marked.

"I have had it with men trying to make me submit and be claimed. I am my own person and wolf for that matter."

"You are just another bitch with special blood to me." The man made the mistake of calling her a bitch again as she bit down, snapping his neck.

"I guess we are done interrogating him then." Aaron huffed as he stepped back from me. My anger had turned my eyes red as blood. He knew that he had to control Kyra before we bolted away. He stepped forward again to put his hand in my main over my star patch.

I instantly felt a calmness and need grow within me. I lay so Aaron can touch me more. He rubbed his face on my muzzle, kissing me gently.

I linked to him to let him know that I was not wearing my gown so I would need clothes. I figured I would really cause a ruckus if I were standing there naked. The other pack members started to come back out as the threat of the rogue's was now over. A surprise attack of children all over my wolf made me jump, sending little bodies rolling. Every single one of them jumped back up and ran back to cuddle into my fur.

Kyra was purring in delight of all the love she was receiving. Little Luke looked right into my eyes, "why are you so big? You are the biggest wolf ever." Kyra licked his face and pushed her muzzle into his belly, causing him to laugh hysterically.

All of the pack members gathered around me to praise me as they all touched me. Ana approached me. "Thank you for saving my son again my Luna. You are the bravest woman I know. Please let me know if you ever need anything. I am eternally grateful to you. Everyone is wanting to touch you because you are the only white wolf that anyone has ever seen. You are special to all of us." Ana grabbed Luke to take him home as he struggled in her arms.

"I want to stay with Natalie though momma. She is my angel."

"You can come visit me anytime Luke. You mind your mother now." He huffed as his Ana carried him off to their house. My heart ached for both of them with having to go through another rogue attack. I was the cause of it though. The thought of these wonderful people getting hurt because of me broke my heart.

Chapter Twelve

The Call for Help

I went to my room to shower immediately after I was able to get away from the children that wanted to play. The game of chase was great fun for a time. I of course got out of the shower to Aaron waiting for me. "Do you ever get tired of watching me shower?" I tilt my head with an eyebrow raised.

"Nope. Never will either. You're just lucky I do have some will power. Otherwise you wouldn't be able to shower alone." He chuckled while giving me the seductive side smile. "You do realize you are a natural Luna. Everyone loves you. You make them feel better and guide them. You are willing to protect the pack by any means necessary."

"I am not a Luna. We are not married."

"Not yet, if I have anything to do with it."

I smile as I cross the room to the closet to get my sleep shirt and underwear. I drop my towel to put on my underwear then shirt. Aaron stood watching me the entire time. I grinned to myself to know I could feel the heat that emanated from his gaze. The control was completely mine.

"Tell you what. You can sleep in the bed with me tonight instead of Jax, if you can control yourself. I do find you rather calming." I smiled as his mouth dropped open without any words.

"You knew about that? Jax thought he was being sneaky. Okay, we both did. I didn't mean to be creepy or anything. We just had to be near you."

"So what are you going to do? I'm going to bed."

Before the last word was out of my mouth he had his shirt off, pants undone while kicking off his socks and shoes.

I climbed in the bed so that the moonlight and stars shone in the window on me. Aaron clad only in his boxers, looked at me curiously. I reached back pulling the covers back for his invitation. He sunk into the bed beside me as I heard a low growl emit from his chest, pulling my body next to his.

He slid his arm under my head as he wrapped his other arm around my waist. "You may need to loosen the grip around my waist some Aaron. I do need to breathe." I chuckled softly as the comfort surrounded me.

"Sorry, I just wanted to make sure you weren't going to escape. I don't ever want to let go of you now." He kissed the back of my shoulder before settling into his pillow. I was relieved that there was some fabric between our bodies.

I let my body relax as I had never relaxed before. I felt like I had melted into my spot as my mind, body, and soul seemed to have decided to get along.

"Goodnight Natalie, my goddess. I love you."

I felt the words and I didn't have my normal reaction. My body stayed relaxed as my mind wandered into a happy place. The contentment kept me relaxed. I didn't respond to him, but I bet that he knew he had a good response.

The dream came shortly after I had faded into the darkness of sleep.

I walked along the open meadow, enjoying the smell of the flowers. The colored popped out as if you could touch them, so vibrant and full of life. The tall grass tickled my ankles as

I wandered along. I looked up into the clear, blue sky, covering my eyes from the bright sun.

The sound of my name drew my attention back to the meadow, directly in front of me. Nana stood a few steps away from me with her arms stretched out to me. Of course I ran to grasp her in a tight embrace. "Be careful with an old woman would you." Her laughter sounded like music to my ears. How I missed her laugh.

"Nana, how is this possible? I have missed you so much. I feel so alone now. What am I going to do without you?" I cried tears of joy and sadness as I refused to let her go.

Nana pulled back from me. "Why are you crying my strong, beautiful girl? I will always be with you. All you have to do is think about me and I will be right there." She smoothed my hair back from my face as she wiped my tears away. Replacing my tears with a kiss on each cheek.

"It isn't the same Nana. I want to talk to you every day, give you a hug every day, and have you talk to me."

"Yet here we are dear. The mate bond is strong enough for you to visit me anytime *you want. He brings you peace of your mind, body, and soul."*

"I don't know what to do though Nana. He rejected me right after we got here, when you…… fell." The tears streamed down my cheeks again with the memory.

"Dear, dear, dear. It was my time to go. If it had not been my time then I would still be there. The Moon Goddess is the one that makes this possible. Our loved ones live on. You keep me alive in the dream realm. I will always be here. There is something coming though. I am here to let you know that you are going to have the power of choice. You are very special as you have learned. You were kept in the dark and hidden because of this reason." Nana laced her fingers with mine. "Walk with me my dear."

"You will have a decision to make. You are coming to the crossroads of your life now. Your powers will be used for good very soon. You will have the answers soon. Choose wisely as you have more free will than most. No decision will be wrong. You need to decide what is best for you." We walked to a stream as we sat on the log.

I glanced around as I could hear a thumping. "What is that Nana? Do you hear it too?"

"Anytime you need me, I will be here waiting for you. I love you my dear Nat. Let love guide you."

I opened my eyes in a panic as the dream ended. Aaron was out of the bed. I lay alone. I sit up, scanning the room to see him standing at the door, talking to someone. He quietly closes the door, turning back to the bed. His look of confusion peaked my interest. "What is going on?"

"A report just came across that there are at least ten Lycan's approaching the pack house. They have been sent here on behalf of the Lycan king. I guess that the rogue's that attacked us had also attacked the castle of the Lycan's." He ran his hands through his hair, staring at me.

"So what does that have to do with anything? I'm not following, I suppose from lack of knowledge."

"They are coming to retrieve you. The king has been mortally wounded and the word has spread about your gift in your blood." He looked mortified. "I can't stop you from going. We are not mated or married. The decision will be yours to go to the realm of the Lycan's. No matter what I say they will take you."

"I wouldn't have to stay there, would I? Why would there be a problem with me going?"

"I would prefer you not to go."

"Why wouldn't you want me to go help the Lycan king?"

"The problem is that you are the only one that will be permitted to enter the realm. No one can go with you. During a time like this, only designated people will be allowed to enter. No matter if you request it. You will have to go alone. I will not be able to go to protect you."

"I can take care of myself. Why would I need to be protected?" I felt myself becoming angry with the thought of him thinking I am too weak to take care of myself.

I got out of the bed and marched to the closet to pack a small bag. One change of clothes, putting on my gown that Greta had made for me. "I am not as weak as you must think I am. If you remember right, I fought alongside the other wolves when we were attacked."

He stomped over to me, grabbing hold of my shoulders, looking into my face. "I don't think you are too weak. I think that you will stand up and fight, not knowing all of the rules may be of dire consequence to you. You are so damn hardheaded." His lips connected to mine in a fierce, yet tender kiss. My body instantly responded to his, opening up to his search of my mouth.

My arms found their way as around his neck as he deepened the kiss farther, a moan escaped my throat. He pulled back putting his hands on either side of my face. "I worry about your safety. You are an unmated, unclaimed, unmarried woman of age. I hate to ask, but you know I love you and would do anything for you. Will you let me mate and claim you before you leave? You are my entire world."

I took a step back, looking at Aaron who was completely serious about his question. The look on my face had to have said it all. My face scrunched up, looking at him like he had three heads. "You were being serious? We haven't even discussed anything of this nature. Do you want me to just throw myself into your arms saying, fuck me and bite me? You haven't even proposed to me. You are out of your fucking mind." I attempted to push past Aaron as he grabbed my arm.

He pulled me against his body. My back to his chest. I felt my body deceive me once again at his mere touch. His mouth came down next to my ear. "I'm sorry my goddess. I fear losing you. I love you so much and I want to do things the right way with you, but you won't talk to me or let me in. If I lose you, I will lose my mind and Jax will destroy everything in his path, including me."

My dream came back to me like another voice yelling in my head of Nana. She said I needed to let someone in. I huffed as I put my head back on his chest. "I will be fine. We can talk when I come back."

He kept his arms wrapped around me as he kissed my head. I felt the calm wash over me. His cheek stay laying on the top of my head as we stood there. A knock came at the door as we knew it was time for me to leave.

Chapter Thirteen

The Lycan Realm

The ten Lycan's were standing in their human form just inside the doors of the pack house. They all looked up the stairwell toward me, bowing as I descended. "There is no need for that." I kind of chuckled. All of the men were taller and more defined than the wolf men. Their size was incredible.

One of the men stepped forward, "Natalie I am pleased to meet you. We are in need of your assistance. King Kylan has sustained moral wounds that we have heard you may be able to assist in healing."

"If you don't mind me saying, you are the perfect image of the Goddess Artemis. You are portrayed as the goddess of the hunt, wilderness, wild animals, chastity, and the moon. I suppose you are a white wolf as well?" His violet eyes sparkled as he looked at me in anticipation.

His gaze wandered around my neck, searching for my marks. His smile spread across his face. "You are of Lycan royalty blood if I am correct. Lycan's can choose mates my lady."

I heard the growl come from behind me as I turned to look Aaron in the eyes. Jax was on the verge of shifting with anger. I put my hand on Aaron's chest over his heart. I heard the moan rattle through his chest with my touch. His eyes now focused on me and not the Lycan. "I will be back. Have I broken my word to you yet? Aaron, Jax." His eyes softened as he leaned in to kiss me tenderly on my lips. As soon as the kiss ended he moved to my neck to place a kiss just below my ear. Where he intended on marking me if he had his choice.

"My goddess. It is time for us to depart. The king awaits your arrival." He held his arm out for me to take. Instead I walked past him out the door. I really didn't want a fight over me touching another man.

When we were all out of the pack house the Lycan's shifted into their form. I watched as I had never seen a Lycan before. They were much larger and stood on their back paws. I willed Kyra forward to shift as all present watched me shift to the large white wolf. The Lycan's stood there looking at me in what must have been amazement. Aaron walks over to me to put his hand in my main, directly over my star as a reminder. Kyra leaned into his touch before groaning.

The Lycan's turned to leave as the lead one looked back at me. I followed him in the lead as the others took up behind me. The darkness that remained of the night kept the Lycan's well hidden. The wind rushed through my fur as we ran for miles. I heard the conversation that they would have occasionally. They didn't know I could hear them. They said at one time that they were impressed with my size and speed. I was more than just a wolf for sure.

We came to a clearing that looked like the place I talked to Nana in my dreams. The exact log we sat on was beside the water. The lead Lycan stopped beside me as the others jumped the stream, disappearing. The portal to the Lycan world was the stream.

The Lycan motioned for me to go through the portal ahead of him. I jumped across the stream to land on the green grass of an entirely new world. The sky was a violet color with the sun rising. "Is the sky always this color?" I linked to the Lycan that looked at me in surprise. "Yes, I can link with anyone I choose to. I thought you knew that until I overheard some of the conversations the other Lycan's were having."

"The skies are always this color. Slightly more pale than right now though. You are definitely special goddess. Follow me to the king."

I observed as much of the realm as I could with our steady pace. The trees of beautiful flowers, different than any I had ever seen before. The tree limbs seemed to move on their own while there was no wind. The castle appeared in the distance. The pure magnificence of the castle before me took my breath away. The castle looked like it was right out of a fairytale book.

The trees surrounding the castle had flowers that looked like they were roses. The aroma of the rose type flowers filled the air and my senses. The sun had come up from behind the castle to reveal not just one, but two suns. They were not as intense as the one I am used to.

"Wait until you see the two moons my goddess. They are magnificent. My name is Donis by the way. Sorry I didn't properly introduce myself. I am the second in charge."

"I may have a lot of questions. I just found out recently about wolves and now Lycans. Please excuse my ignorance. I am a quick learner though."

"If you are disrespected in any form or fashion please tell me. They will have to deal with me if so."

We entered the main gates of the castle. The rock walls were covered in flowering vines, making a maze of flowers up the walls. The water fountains of different, what appeared to be gods and goddesses flowed with crystal clear water that sparkled in the rays of the suns.

The stairway up to the large wood doors of the castle opened as we approached. Donis shifted back to his human form as I followed suit. "We had a robe prepared for your shift. I have never seen a wolf that could shift back to human form that did not have to redress themselves."

"I have a special gown that allows for me to shift and remain dressed. A good friend of mine Greta made it special for me."

"You mean the right hand of the goddess herself? Greta is always by the side of the Moon Goddess. She is known as a pearl. She resembles the full moon." He stood there with a questioning look on his face as the look on my face was probably that of utter confusion.

"I guess I would need to get back to you on that one. I have no idea." I am starting to think that maybe I am in the middle of another dream. This has to be.

"Goddess, are you ready to meet the king? He is anxiously awaiting your arrival.

The great room we entered was filled with tapestries and painting. There was a staircase to either side of the great hall. In the middle of the great room there was a statue of the Moon Goddess. The statue was stunning with detail. Her beauty was portrayed with such elegance.

Before our ascent up the staircase to the right, Donis stops in front of a beautiful painting of a woman. I looked closely as it looked like it was a painting of myself. The woman in the painting had a star on her neck just as I do. Exact same spot even. I gasped at the uncanny similarity between us.

"Do you see what I mean now goddess?"

"Why do you continue to call me goddess? You referred to me by my human name of Natalie."

"You are the reincarnate of the Goddess Artemis. You are a goddess, Natalie. You are a goddess to the wolves and the Lycan's. The wolves may not have the information as far back to realize who you are. The elders may realize who you are if they looked into the history more."

Donis continued his ascent up the grand staircase with me in tow of him. He stopped and asked me to walk beside him. "You are a goddess and should not follow have to follow any."

I took my place beside the man that was probably almost a foot taller than myself. "I must ask though, why does the Goddess Artemis have a star on her neck?" As I rubbed the scar on my neck.

We continued to walk as he told me the story. "Mankind captured the goddess. Her powers were thought to be evil as per most humans don't understand the powers of the Gods. It is said that the Moon

Goddess sent a star to capture Artemis before her demise. The star entered her neck there bringing her to the home of the Gods."

"I got my scar on my neck from a car accident years ago from a piece of glass from my car window. Mine is not from a star." I laughed as we continued to walk.

Donis stopped. He looked at me very seriously. "May I touch the scar on your neck goddess?"

"I suppose you can. I have never had that kind of request before. I guess it won't hurt anything."

Donis reached his hand toward my neck slowly as he laid the palm of his large hand over my scar. A sudden jolt moved his body as he quickly withdrew his hand from me. I stood there looking at him in shock. A strange pulse ran through my veins as he stared at me.

"The power that comes from within you is too much for me to touch you. I felt as if I could not breathe. You are without a doubt the Goddess Artemis." He bowed down to me again. I touched his shoulder gently. A growl emanated from his chest as his eyes darkened with him looking back up at me. "Dear goddess your touch stirs something in me that I have never experienced. You should not touch anyone that you are going to have as a chosen mate." He stood and cleared his throat.

"I do not mean to be rude. Please don't take what I say as so. Your purity makes you completely irresistible. You stir my beast."

I stepped back from him as I felt my cheeks flush. I think I may have flushed from my toes all the way up to my cheeks. How could he possibly know that? I smiled as to cover my flush as much as possible. I didn't know how to even start to respond to his comments.

Chapter Fourteen

Lycan King

I continued to walk in the direction we had been going as so I didn't have to respond or think about the conversation. I turned my attention once again to the paintings on the walls. A breeze rushed past me with the smell of roses. I lifted my head to inhale deeply as we approached a room at the end of the corridor.

Donis opened one of the large doors of the two, ushering me inside. I avoided making any contact with him. He seemed to breathe a sigh of relief as we entered the kings chambers. The massive room was decorated in the most intricate wood carved furniture I have ever seen.

The aroma of the roses continued to tickle at my senses as a man that was the most beautiful specimen I had ever laid my eyes on walked out of the bathroom. The breeze rushed past my hair once more, my strands of hair moved with the force. The open windows didn't show any signs of a breeze. No movement in the curtains at all.

I looked over to the king once more for his neon blue eyes to be piercing my eyes. He slightly bowed to me, almost falling. I ran to his side to assist him back into the bed before he fell. Donis assisted me to get him back into the bed. The man was so much larger than I was. I couldn't have assisted him without help.

"I am King Kylan. You are my goddess that I have been waiting for." His eyes seemed to become heavier as he spoke.

"What are your wounds King Kylan? How can I help you?" I looked over his body quickly to see a blood stain on his shirt, over the ribcage on the left. My instincts as a nurse kicked in as I pulled his shirt up to expose the wound.

I exposed more than just a wound. The most perfect male specimen of chest and stomach was at my fingertips. I felt a rush of warmth run through my veins like fire as my hand lay on his body. I quickly pull my hand away to look at Donis. "I need you to get me hot water and a small blade."

Kylan reached over, grabbing my hand. He put my hand back on his chest over his heart, covering my hand with his own. "Your touch takes the pain away. Please continue to touch me." I stood there not knowing what to say as I looked at the wound to keep my mind busy.

Donis returned to the room with a couple other women in tow to help with whatever it was I needed to get done. A smaller pretty girl handed me a washcloth that had been in the clean warm water. "Thank you. Please have another ready to wash and then a bandage to cover the wound."

She nodded her head at me as she bowed at the same time. I looked to the other girl that bowed to me as well. They left the room to obtain the bandages I requested.

I washed the wound that was oozing blood. The blood was flowing freely, he was losing too much blood. His face became more pale. "Donis, I need the small blade."

Donis reached for his blade on his side. He handed the blade to me handle first with a questioning look on his face. I used the other warm wet cloth to wipe my hand on. I ran the blade across my palm.

The twinge of pain made me intake my breath. Kalen watched every move I made as he reached for me to touch him.

Kalen grabbed hold of my arm holding it tenderly. "I can touch you and it helps too."

I placed my hand over the wound so that my blood was going into the wound. The oozing of the blood stopped. My instincts told me that there was more that I would need to do on this type of wound.

I looked to Kalen that was staring at me. "I need you to touch the star on my neck. Put your palm over it." He reached across himself to place his palm over the scar on my neck. "Don't move your hand until I tell you to."

Kalen placed his hand over my scar as his eyes widened. He continued to stare into my eyes as I pushed a little harder on the wound to release more of my blood. The pulse of power flowed from my body and into his hand. He closed his eyes as I lifted my hand. My blood dripped onto the wound that was now healing over.

I closed my hand into a fist to stop the bleeding. "Bandage please." I said to the girl. She handed me the bandage that I wrapped around my hand. The room started to narrow in around my vision. The pulsing stopped between his hand and my neck. "You can take your hand away now please."

Kalen moved his hand away from my neck as I blinked several times to stop the hot flashes coming over me as the tunnel of darkness consumed me. I collapsed onto the floor.

Donis was leaning over to pick me up as Kalen spoke. "Don't touch her. I am the only one to touch her. She is the Goddess Artemis. She is mine." He sat up, taking off his shirt with blood on it to cradle her on his chest. She looked so petite compared to his body. He relished in the comfort that washed over him. The scent of something different but sweet invaded his senses, coming from Natalie.

The girls quickly changed the bed as Kalen held Natalie against his chest. "She will be queen. She is meant to be my queen." He looked lovingly on her face as she slept in his arms. "Donis, I want you to make sure to prepare a celebration for tonight. I am back from the brink of death, and I have found my queen."

"I should let you know that she has a mate in the human world with an alpha wolf. He has not laid claim to her. I got the feeling that she is not receptive to having a mate. She does have the mate bond with him though."

Kylan growled at Donis as he gripped her tighter to himself. "I guess we will see whom she chooses then. She has the ability to choose her mate with being a goddess. I need to convince her to stay here with me."

After the bed was changed and ready he laid Natalie gently into his bed. It took every bit of control he had to not claim her at this moment. If he laid claim to her then she would stay for sure. The mark of the Lycan would leave the mate bond unbreakable between them, not to mention she would then be Lycan and not wolf. He knew he had to let her make the choice though.

I opened my eyes slowly as I remember fainting after I healed Kylan. My head hurt slightly. I rubbed the side of my head, realizing that I was lying in a bed that smelled of the roses. A fresh breeze blew over me. I turned to the windows to be able to admire the scent even more to see Kylan standing in front of the window, looking at me with a smile.

"I'm happy to see you are awake my queen. I have something for you to drink to make your head quit hurting." He handed me a gold goblet with a foul-smelling substance inside.

"It does taste just as terrible as it smells, but it will make the pain go away. I promise." His smile made me feel better. He ran his hand over my forehead into my hair. I didn't pull away from his touch like I usually do. I was surprised even with myself.

I drank down the bitter liquid in one gulp. "That is terrible, just like you said it would be." I shook my head from the taste that remained in my mouth.

"I can fix that for you too." Kylan leaned over placing his lips on mine. I didn't move at first from the shock of the kiss. My body responded on its own. I opened my mouth, returning the kiss that he deepened with his tongue discovering the depths of my mouth. The bitter taste in my mouth was replaced by a sweet mint flavor.

My brain realized what was happening as my hands touched his chest. I pulled away, looking at him as he stood over me. He seemed to have a glow to his skin. The shimmer of his lips caught my attention. I looked away as to not think about the kiss that I just had with a complete stranger.

I sat up to realize I was wearing a white gown. "Where is my gown I was wearing?"

"Your gown was covered in blood my queen. I sent it to be washed for you. I have a gown here for you to wear." He motioned toward the wardrobe where a beautiful dark red gown of a satin hung. "There is to be a celebration in your honor tonight. I was hoping you would wear this gown my queen."

"Why do you keep calling me your queen? I have been called Goddess all day and now queen."

"You are my mate and to be the rightful queen." He smiled brightly at me. "I know you feel the bond and smell the scent of me as I do you too. We are meant to be together. I understand that a wolf has a mate bond with you as well. You my queen have the ability to make your choice of mate." He approached the side of the bed again to kneel next to me.

"Will you marry me and become my queen?" He extended a box with a large diamond, staring in my eyes.

"I..... um..... I can't answer that question. I just met you. I have only lived

with my human side my entire life. I don't
let my heart lead my mind around." My
thoughts went to Aaron. I had just had this
conversation with him. I go from a quiet
reserved life to two men wanting me.

Kylan looks into my eyes with more
love than he had before. I am confused by
his reaction. Not what I was expecting.
"Then I suppose we need to get to know
one another better. I have nothing but time
to wait for my queen to decide." He placed
a hand to the side of my face. I felt the
electricity move within every nerve ending
his hand touched. How can this be? How
can I have two mates?

Life just became more confusing
than it already had been.

I had been sleeping for most of the
day. The suns were setting on the last rays
of the day. The violet sky was more vivid
than it had been with the rising of the sun.
My body remained somewhat weak as I

decided to get dressed into the dress that Kylan had asked me to wear.

The echoes of the dream resonated within my head. I must make a choice. I now have two men that begged for my love. I had never loved a man ever, besides my father that was taken from me.

The celebration in my honor was to be held in the courtyard of the castle. The beauty of the landscape from the window of the castle made me yearn to explore everything it had to offer.

I slipped the gown of satin over my head as it slinked down my body with a wiggle of my hips. The spaghetti straps held the dress in the perfect position. My athletic build looked amazing in the gown. The full-length mirror reflected a new side of me. I hardly recognized the person looking back at me.

I seemed to have a shimmer to my skin. My mind wandered to the fact that I had mixed blood with the Lycan king. I may have used my power and magic within, but so did he. I ran my fingers over my collarbone to make sure the reflection was my own. I wore my hair down but pushed over my shoulder to somewhat hide my scar.

I sense I am not alone, looking in the mirror to the reflection behind me. Kylan stands a foot taller than myself behind me. He steps so close to me that I can feel the heat of his body on my back. "I have something for you to wear with that gown my queen." He lowers a dazzling necklace over my head to my neck.

The rubies and diamonds sparkle as the cool metal and stones touch my skin. The precious stones hold some kind of power as tingling starts in my nerve endings. "What kind of power does this necklace hold? I can feel it."

"This necklace holds the jewels of the previous queens of the Lycans. Direct descendants of the Moon Goddess." He smiled as he finished doing the clasp. I felt the power coursing through my veins. Kyra howled as she felt the surge of power run through us like a freight train.

A glow emanated from around my body. The violet glow is dim but present. Kylan lowers his lips to my neck, placing a kiss over my scar. My body sparked with a fire that tightened my core with need. I clenched my legs together tighter to control the feeling. He continued to kiss and run his tongue over my neck. His whispers reach my ear, the language I don't understand, starts to translate in my mind. The words unfolding in my mind.

My head had fallen to the side as the assault on my senses continues. The words he whispered now hit my mind. "My queen you are the most beautiful being. I will claim you and make you mine. Your white wolf will become the white Lycan as I mark you." The feel of the points of his canine teeth bring my mind to reality.

My eyes fly open as I move in the opposite direction of Kylan. "I am not ready for anything like that. It is going to take me a little bit of time to make such a big decision."

Everything seems to come down to me being claimed by a man. Why must I be claimed? Why can't I just freely choose to be with someone? I feel like I will become a possession more than an equal. I have always been independent, relying only on myself. I can take care of myself just fine. I am really liking the attention I have deprived myself of for years, but this is just getting ridiculous. Every time I turn around a male is attempting to claim me.

It will be my choice as to whom I would like to stay with. I have all of the reactions to them. Why is that not enough for them to be happy that I choose them? I will never understand this claiming shit as long as I live.

I still have so many questions as to what is going on in my life, let alone choosing between these two men now. Not a single one of them has asked me what I want. What my heart desires.

Kylan stood there without moving. His eyes reflected the rejection he just felt from me. "I'm sorry. I need more time. I feel the bond with you. I am confused and so new to the situation. I have so many questions. Please understand."

"I do understand. I will give you the time you need my queen. I'm sorry that the beast within myself craves you so much that it is as struggle. Please be patient with me as well."

I smiled to Kylan with his request for me to be patient as well. "I will remember that my king."

"I love the sound of that coming from your lips my queen."

Chapter Fifteen

In Honor of the Goddess

Kylan dressed in his tailored suit with a robe of red extended his arm for me to take. "My queen, we have an event to attend in your honor. May I escort you?" His smile said everything that had come from his lips. The man had the charm of any king in a fairytale. I wrapped my arm through the crook of his arm.

We exited the room to have people who bowed as we left the room. Kylan would politely nod to all who bowed to us. The grand staircase came into view as we approached the landing. The large room was full of people waiting to greet us. The entire crowd bowed down, as did Kylan to me.

I stood in shock as if a statue. Kylan then the rest of the crowd stood. The remarks were all murmured as the crowd whispered to each other. We descended the stairs to the crowd parting for us to move through to the great doors, standing open for us.

The courtyard was full of lights as we exited the castle. The glow of the lights made the area magical. A large table sat among the roses. Kylan walked me to the head of the table to pull a chair out. The two chairs that sat at the head of the table were of magnificent carvings with a red velvet. The scene was looking more and more like it was out of a fairytale.

We stood in front of our chairs as the crowd found places to sit. Two chalices of wine were brought to us before we all sat. Kylan raised his chalice up as the crowd followed suit. "I would like to welcome the Goddess Artemis Natalie to our home. She is the ultimate reason for my life at this time. All honor her for her gift of life and hopefully to become your queen."

The crowd cheered as I held up my chalice as well. The wine was the sweetest I had ever drank. No bitterness at all. I drank the wine as if my thirst could not be quenched. Everyone ate and drank as the conversations and laughter filled the night air.

I felt the hairs on the back of my neck and arms prickle. I looked around in confusion. An owl hooted in the distance as the trees seem to speak to me. Kylan looks to me with confusion on his face. "What is the problem my queen? Something bothers you?"

"Something is wrong. I feel it." I continued to focus on the surrounding area. "Something is very wrong." I stand up scanning more intently. "Get the warriors on the ready. I think another attack is coming." The crowd stopped with their laughter and talking to listen to me. "Get all of the women and children into the castle. NOW!" I scream. The woman and children start moving for the castle as the first of the rogue Lycan's jump out of the surrounding trees to attack a guard.

Kyra takes the front as I shift into my wolf. The large white wolf has hackles up, teeth bared. Kylan shifts next to me into his Lycan form. I turn around just in time to avoid a Lycan lunging toward me. I sidestep for the rogue to tumble past me. Kyra snarls at the Lycan as it focuses on me once again. Kylan lunged at the rogue to prevent the attack on me.

The other Lycan grabs something from the table as he focuses on Kylan this time. Kylan attempts to move away from the advance as the rogue fakes his movement to plunge a knife into the heart of Kylan. I hit the rogue from the side to send him reeling into motion from my hit.

The knife remained lodged in Kylan's chest. As I was looking at him the rogue lunges at me with his teeth bared. His teeth graze across my shoulder, just missing my neck. The blood runs down my arm as I continue to avoid the lunges. The pain searing in my shoulder.

From behind I am attacked by two other rogues that hold me down. My blood is pooling in the spot I lay as the weakness threatens to take over, making me pass out. My eyes dart to see Kylan is dead. I feel the sting of the tears, that spill in the realization that he is gone. Now I understand why Aaron did what he did. The pain in my heart threatened to take my breath away. I struggle more as the tunnel vision of the two magnificent full moons overhead is the last thing I see.

"Something is wrong with Natalie. I just know it. I can feel it." Aaron paces in his office. "She has been gone too long and I feel pain coming from her. She might be in another realm, but I feel it."

"I need to get to her. I don't know how, but I have to do it now. She is in danger."

"What do you propose we do Aaron? Storm into the Lycan realm demanding them to give your mate back? We would be cut down quicker than you could get the words out."

"I am going to go to the portal of the Lycan realm to see if things are okay. I will take ten of the men with me. You will be in charge while I am gone." He ran his hand through his hair as the frustration coursed through his mind.

The link had been sent out to the other warriors in the pack to get ready to travel, possibly battle for his goddess to be brought home. His mind wandered to the image of Natalie's face, the feel of her skin, the sound of her breathing as she slept peacefully in his arms.

Aaron and the other wolves shifted to get to the realm portal quicker. The hard run did some good to clear his mind some. Jax was at the front with a vengeance to get Natalie back.

The pack of wolves enter into the meadow of the portal to see a man lying on the ground near the stream. Aaron approached the man cautiously. He circled the man sniffing at him. The man was definitely a Lycan. He slightly moved, looking up at Aaron.

Aaron shifted into his human form so he could speak to the man. His heart sank at the sight of a Lycan on the verge of death by the realm. It is very difficult to actually kill a Lycan.

"The king is dead. She warned us that the attack was coming. We fought the rogue Lycan's. They caught us by surprise at the supper in honor of the Goddess Artemis Natalie. She had saved the life of the king for it to be taken again." He coughed on the blood that choked his throat.

"What about Natalie? What happened to her?" Aaron impatient for an answer.

"I saw at least three rogues take her down. I couldn't save her from them. I barely made it here to try and get help from the Lycan's that reside on this side of the realm. Donis will become the new king. We need to get help in there for him. I don't know what happened to him. I didn't see him."

"Let's get him back to the pack house so we can contact the Lycan's in this realm to help. We obviously can't go in there now." Aaron tried to connect to Natalie. "I'm coming for you my goddess. I love you."

As the boundaries of the pack came into view they notified the doctor that he was needed. The doctor was ready as they brought the Lycan man into the office. "My name is Collum." He spoke briefly before he lost consciousness. The doctor performed his examination as he obtained a vile of blood from the refrigerator.

"Natalie wanted to make sure we had some blood on hand if it was needed. I hope this works." He dripped several drops of the blood from the vial onto the chest wound of Collum. The wound started to heal over as he opened his eyes. The wound disappeared before their eyes.

Collum stood from the table running his hand over the wound that had been on his chest. Only the scars remained of his wound. "Is that the blood of the Goddess? We had heard that she had healed the king in the same manner. We have all seen a miracle with the return of the Goddess."

"What are you talking about when you speak of Natalie and her being a Goddess?" Aaron knew that he considered her his goddess, but not that she truly was a goddess.

"Natalie is the reincarnate of the Goddess Artemis. She is the goddess of the hunt, the wilderness, wild animals, chastity, and the moon. She even bears the mark of the Goddess on her neck. Most wolves are not as educated for the ancients as we Lycan's are."

"I need to contact the Lycan clans in your realm. I hope that the Goddess has lived. She has probably been marked by the rogue already that planned the attack to capture her."

Aaron yelled as Jax shifted instantly. The thought of someone else claiming his mate made his anger boil over in frustration. John stood next to Jax talking to him calmly. "Jax, we will get your mate back. She will be fine. Calm down so we can come up with a plan to go get her."

Collum stood back watching as Jax relaxed slightly. Aaron was able to take control back this time to shift back to his human form. "I had no idea that she had a wolf mate. She did not bear any marks. I know that King Kylan made it clear that Natalie was his mate and hoped for her to become queen. He had not marked her."

Aaron seethed with anger again. He was able to control Jax from taking over again. The words rang in his head that he had not marked her. That means that she didn't submit to him. That's his girl. She is to be cherished and earned. Not pushed into something she didn't want.

Collum, Aaron and John went to Aaron's office so he could call the other Lycan's. The plan was to meet in the meadow at the portal the next day at dark. They knew they needed the element of surprise on their side.

Jax paced inside the mind of Aaron. "We can't wait that long. She is in pain and needs us now. We must go to her. I need her back here with me." Aaron felt the same but knew he needed to keep Jax calm, otherwise he would ruin the plan to get Natalie back. "We are not a one-man army Jax. We need the help of the Lycan's right now." Jax snarled as he stopped pacing to retreat.

Aaron continued to try and reach Natalie with a link. No success. He could only hope that maybe she had heard him that he was coming to rescue her, bring her home.

My head pounded as I attempted to open my eyes. I focused on the vision of Aaron to calm myself some. It brought a minute of solace to my mind, reducing the pain slightly. I opened one eye very slowly, looking around the best I could. All I could see was darkness.

I lay in the bed of Kylan. What happened? Why am I here? This is the kings chambers. The memory of Kylan having a knife protruding from his chest came crashing down. I felt the sting of the tears with the thought. He was such a beautiful gentle man. He died saving my life.

The pain in my shoulder brought my attention back fully when I attempted to move it. I know that wolves heal fast, but when you are wounded by a Lycan it takes longer to heal. The blood no longer seeped. A bandage is in place to cover it. My entire body is sore and stiff. How long had I been laying here? Why am I laying in here, in this bed if the rogue's attacked us.

I sit up slightly, fighting through the searing pain in my right shoulder. The door opens as Donis walks through the door wearing the crown and robe that Kylan once wore. "My dear Natalie, you are awake. I have been so worried about you." He leaned over to place a kiss on my forehead as he sat on the edge of the bed looking at me.

"You must be so thirsty and hungry." He motioned for the man that came in with him to go get the water and food. "I saved you from the rogue Lycan's. I saw several of them attack you after Kylan was killed. I rushed to your aid, rescuing you from the beasts. You had collapsed, I think they hit you in the head or something. The rogue was going to mark you as I stopped him just in time. I'm sorry but I had to claim you to get them to stop the attack. After I marked you they must have decided that they had no reason to be here any longer."

I reach up to my neck to feel the puncture marks on my left side. Not over my scar. I felt the stinging of the tears threatening to fall from my eyes. "Kylan is dead then?"

"Yes Natalie. He was dead when I had gotten to you. I checked him, hoping by some miracle he was alive.

"How long have I slept?"

"You have been sleeping almost all day. The attack was last night. I assume with the Lycan change from wolf, that you needed your rest."

"What do you mean Lycan change from wolf?"

"Once a wolf or person is marked by a Lycan they themselves become Lycan. You are no longer a wolf but a Lycan, and hopefully my queen. I intend to have you by my side with my mark."

"So I am now a Lycan and not a wolf?"

"You will transform to a Lycan and then it will be permanent, but not until you change the first time to Lycan. Your wolf is probably going through the changes now to become Lycan." Donis ran his hand down her cheek with a smile.

Chapter Sixteen

Rescuing Natalie

Aaron and Jax paced all night long. Aaron had laid in Natalie's bed to be able to smell her scent. A calm would come over him that soon dissipated with the thoughts of her gone. He dreamed of her in the short spirts that he slept, feeling worse than when he had gone to sleep. After many futile attempts he gave up the attempt to sleep.

The men were all ready as they left in the morning to get to the realm at the setting of the sun. The Lycan's were there waiting for our arrival. One by one they shifted into their Lycan forms. The wolves followed suit. They all jumped into the portal for the Lycan's to form a circle around the pack of wolves.

The castle came into view as the night descended into the valley. The Lycan's were eager to get to the castle just as much as Aaron was. His mate was there, and their king had been slain. Hopefully, there were no more rogue's present.

One of the Lycan's, Collum, had gone ahead of the others to inspect and survey the area. "The area is quiet. There is nothing going on. I spoke to one of the guards that said Donis is now the king, and he does have Natalie with himself. Aaron, I want you to listen very carefully." The large black wolf looked up at him.

"Donis was there at the tail end of the attack, and he did mark Natalie." He grabbed Jax around the throat as three other wolves piled on him to keep him from reaping havoc on the plan. "I need you to focus Aaron. I need you to work with us, control your anger." He relaxed his body as Jax whined from frustration, anger, and a broken heart.

"Remember that she is a goddess and can choose her mate. Just because she is marked it doesn't mean that all is said and done. I need you to keep your anger in control. You need a clear mind for this."

The plan to continue made Aaron and Jax focus more. Not all is lost. She is our strong, hardheaded girl. She will be fine. We will see her soon.

They approached the castle gates with Collum in the lead. He had shifted back to his human form to be able to talk to us. The other Lycan's had formed a circle around the wolves. Ten Lycan's and ten wolves marched through the gates. "We have come to see the king. These wolves were found at the portal of the realm. We captured them as they came through the portal." A guard nodded his head as he turned going up the stairs into the castle.

Another of the guards came over to talk to Collum. "So, are you with the new king or not?"

"What do you mean? I have been guarding at the gates of the portal."

"King Donis is thought to be the one responsible for the rogue attack. He was not seen at all until the end of the attack when he claimed the goddess."

Jax started to growl and snarl at the comment by the guard. Collum looked back at him, with a hard look. "Control yourself wolf." Turning back to the guard to obtain as much information as he could.

"Everyone is on the side of the Goddess for sure. She saved many lives. She seemed to know when the attack was coming. She had saved King Kylan and there was a celebration in her honor when this all happened. We were all told by Donis that the threat is now gone."

"That is odd that he would automatically say the threat was gone immediately following an attack. So where is the Goddess now?"

"I was told that she was brought to the chambers of the king after the attack. He is claiming that he saved her from a sure death to keep the people happy. She is a hero to all of the people."

"It does sound like she is a hero, saving all of the women and children like she did. She is truly queen material." A low growl emitted from behind Collum. He put his hands behind his back to indicate for Aaron to calm down.

"I do need my gown please Donis. I can't march around here naked, now can I?" I laughed to make a calm atmosphere.

For some reason, his story was not adding up to Natalie.

"Of course my queen. I will leave you to get ready for something to eat. We will continue the celebration in your honor inside the castle. I have some business to attend to." A guard opened the door motioning for Donis to come to the door.

"I didn't want to upset the queen my king. There have been some intruder wolves captured at the portal of the realm. They are outside the castle right now."

"I will come out with you now. The queen is needing a moment to herself." Donis casted another glance to Natalie before he left the room in a rush. He figures that the wolves are more than likely the alpha and his men looking for Natalie.

An evil smile crossed his face as he knew what he would have to do to keep Natalie to himself. He would have to have Aaron killed in front of Natalie to prove that she will need to stay with him.

I quickly got out of the bed as the room spun with my quick movements. I retrieved my gown that Greta had made for me. I would need to have it for tonight. Something was very wrong. I felt as if Aaron and Jax were close. I thought maybe I was imagining things. "Aaron or Jax are you there?"

Jax perked his ears up as the link from Natalie came across. "We are here Natalie. You have no idea how happy we are that you are okay."

"You have no idea how happy I am to hear your voice. I am in a mess here. You warned me and I didn't listen, but we will talk about that later. Donis is the king now and there is something off. His story is not right for some reason. Something is wrong."

"We are here in the castle right now. I need you to do something that is going to kill me more than you know. I need you to act like you don't want anything to do with me and you want to be with him. Can you do that for me my goddess?"

"Why would I do that Aaron?"

"We are here with some Lycan's from our realm. We have a plan. I need you to do this for me. I love you so much Natalie."

"I will do it. I have decided something though."

"What is that my goddess?"

"I love you too Aaron and don't forget Jax."

Aaron and Jax were hardly able to hold their excitement back as the words echoed for them. The day they have waited for, has finally come.

Collum looked back at Jax. Jax nodded his head to him to signal that Natalie knew what her part was in the upcoming events. Collum then linked to Aaron. "I do need you to tell her something else. If she shifts to Lycan before you have marked and mated her she will remain a Lycan. You will need to mark and mate her as soon as you can."

"Natalie. I do need to give you more information."

"What is it Aaron?"

"You cannot shift until after I mark and mate you as a wolf. If you shift before then, you will remain a Lycan. I'm sorry I have to give you this news right now of all times."

"I understand Aaron."

Chapter Seventeen

Plans in Motion

Donis descended the stairs of the castle to the group of Lycan's and wolves waiting for him. "Well, we meet again, alpha Aaron. I really hope you are here to wish Natalie the best in our upcoming wedding. I have claimed the Goddess as my own."

Jax snarled and lunged toward Donis as the Lycan's held him back. Jax wanted to rip his throat out and watch him choke to death on his own blood for what he had done to Natalie.

"Good job men for capturing these intruders. They will be put to death for such treacherous actions." He looked back to the wolves. "You will shift to your human form now. I can't stand the smell of wet dogs." Donis nodded his head as a young woman threw a pile of pants to the group.

The pack of wolves shifted to their human form. The Lycan's did not so he would not see faces he didn't recognize.

Aaron lunged at Donis after he put his pants on. He didn't get to him before the Lycan's stopped his attack. "Take them to the dungeon's until I call for them." Donis smirked as he turned walking away. "I have plans to complete before the celebration and my marriage. I will be busy. Don't bother me."

The Lycan's motioned for the pack members to follow them. They complied with being taken to the dungeons per the plan.

They walked around the castle to the outside entrance for the dungeons. Looking around they were alone. Collum grabs Aarons' arm, pushing him into the bushes. They had no idea if the guards in the dungeons were true to Donis or not. He motioned for Aaron to stay there.

The tunnel into the dungeon was poorly lit. The guards on duty knew that they were receiving prisoners. They had the metal bars of the holding cell open for them to enter. "I will be back when the king requests their presence." The guard nodded in acknowledgement.

The Lycan's exit the opening for the dungeons to motion for Aaron to follow. Collum was taking Aaron up to where Natalie was being held. There was a secret escape route that led directly to the king's chambers. Collum had been part of the king's detail, so he knew about the secret passage.

The passage had never been used so the metal gate was difficult to open at first. The passage was dark and spiraled. The passage connected to the wardrobe in the bathroom. Collum shifted back to his human form as he was too large to fit through the opening.

"The wardrobe is in the bathroom. Once you are through the wardrobe be careful to make sure that Natalie is alone. I don't think there is anyone in there with her though. Lock the main doors. I will keep a watch from the inside near the chamber doors."

Aaron went through the wardrobe to look around. Natalie lay on the bed turned from him. The room was empty except for her. He let Collum know that she was alone. Collum turned in the small space to go back out and into the castle.

Aaron peeked out the bathroom door again to get Natalie's attention. She turned over as she heard the sounds of someone in the bathroom. She jumped up out of the bed to go running to Aaron. He crushed his lips to Natalie's to let her know how he felt about her. She moaned into his mouth as the kiss deepened. He pulled back for a second to put his finger over his lips. She covered her mouth as Aaron made his way to the door to place the wood slat in the notches, locking the doors.

He turned around to have Natalie right there behind him. His body hummed with excitement at the nearness of her. He scooped her up into his arms as their lips connected.

I had a fever burning inside my body with Aaron touching me. I welcomed his kiss as I greedily returned it. Aaron laid me on the bed as his weight came over me. His mouth next to my ear made a rush of excitement and heat pool in my core. I could feel the pressure that begged for him to relieve it.

He grabbed the bottom of my dress, pulling it up and over my head. His gaze held mine. He whispered to me. "I love you Natalie. I want and need you so much. Tell me you want this, want me." His mouth came down to kiss my neck as he waited for my confirmation. He wanted my words, not just my actions.

"I have wanted you since I met you. I need you to put this fire out that you have raging within me." He growled into my ear, causing the tingle to ignite the fire even further.

"I want to worship every inch of you, but we are not able to right now. I love you so much. When we get home you will have nothing but pleasure to replace our time apart." His body trembled with the need for me as I ran my hands over his hard chest and stomach. I could feel the evidence of his need for me, pushing at me.

"This is my first time." I blushed as he kissed my neck.

"I know my goddess. I will be gentle with you, I promise." His hand went to my core to feel how wet and ready I was for him. He grabbed my leg, bringing it up as he pushed the tip into the heat that begged for him. He leaned his body over mine to look into my eyes. "I love you." His mouth covered mine in a demanding yet passionate kiss that took my breath away. He pushed slowly into my core as he met the resistance.

His lips on mine, "I love you Natalie." He pushed past as he absorbed the gasp of pain and pleasure from me. He stopped as he completely filled and stretched me to the limits. I relaxed my body as he moved again. His growl in my ear drove my body to the point of madness as the pain was replaced by the pleasure of our union.

He groaned with every movement. The pressure he was applying to my clit had a pressure building to the point of explosion. I opened my mouth wide as the spiraling explosions happened inside of my body. His mouth came over mine. He moved quicker as his hand replaced his mouth.

"I love you so much Natalie. I am going to claim you. Everything in my life leads me to this moment. His canine teeth emerged as he sank his teeth into my tender flesh over my scar. I arched my back in absolute pleasure with another explosion inside my core. His body spasmed with his release at that moment. The waves of ecstasy continued as he kept his teeth in my neck. The pain and the pleasure of him marking and claiming me was an ecstasy of its own.

I felt the power coursing through my veins as his coursed through me as well. In one last thrust of his body he retracted his teeth from my neck. The power that he shared with me now ran in his veins. His head fell back as he went to release his ecstasy. I reached up to cover his mouth, pulling his mouth down to mine. The kiss was nothing I can explain besides the alpha power and his new power combined. I felt more love than I had ever in my life. I knew then that I had made the right choice.

His body relaxed on mine as we remained together. He started to get soft again as I felt the emptiness starting. "I much prefer the fullness of you." I whispered into his ear. "I can definitely get used to this."

His body moves slightly as he laughs softly kissing my neck that was now just a scar over my other scar. "You really need to see this star on you now. It looks amazing." He raised up onto his elbows to allow me to breathe as he traced the scar on my neck. "Your star is now connected."

He rolled over to my side as I got up to go take a shower. "I need to shower before he comes back and can smell you on me." As I moved to sit up, he noticed the scars that now remained on my shoulder. I heard a low growl emit from deep in his chest.

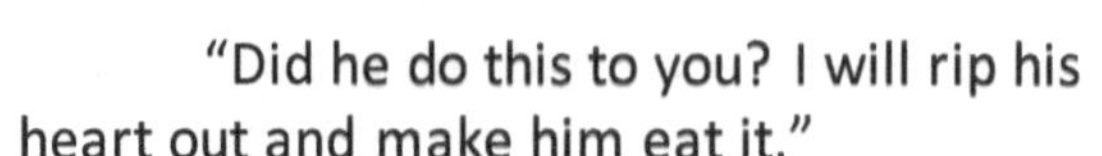

"Did he do this to you? I will rip his heart out and make him eat it."

"I think it was him. I think he is the Lycan that killed Kylan. He had claimed me on the other side of my neck. Thank god he didn't get the other side." I turned my head to show him, but no marks remained. "They are gone, thank god."

Aaron kept his hand over the scars on my shoulder for a few more moments. "I must leave you now my goddess. The plan does not include me being found in bed with you." He laughed softly. "I will see you soon, I love you." He kissed the scars on my shoulder.

"I love you too Aaron." I smiled at him. He came up quickly, crushing his lips to mine.

I walked into the bathroom, starting the shower. "You always watch me shower. It will be weird that you aren't here to watch." I chuckled to him.

"I will see you soon my love. Remember what I told you earlier." Aaron exits out of the wardrobe.

I took my time in my shower. I had just gotten out when I realized that the sheets would give away the fact that I was walking funny for a reason. My gown slid over my body as I went into the room to retrieve the sheets. There was a small amount of blood on the sheets that I expected. The mere size of him would have made me bleed. I was sore in all the right ways though.

I undid the lock from the door so as to not look too suspicious. I took the sheets into the bathroom, putting them on the shower. I knelt beside the tub to wash the blood out as I felt a presence behind me. I turned quickly to see Donis standing in the doorway. "Why do I smell blood from your personal area?"

"I um started, you know. My monthly."

"That is not the smell of that. You have come into heat, my queen. I can smell the arousal in the air." He lifted his head to smell the air.

I tried to play dumb. I didn't know what to say to him. I just knew if I didn't get farther away from him that he would try to claim me. "Is everything ready? I am famished." I got up to push past him as he grabbed me from behind, wrapping his arms around me.

"I promise that once you are my wife I will be gentle when I claim you. I have nothing but love for you my queen. I have wanted you since the moment I saw you." He inhaled the smell of my hair. "You are going to drive me crazy, my queen. I want you so much right now."

"Well, you need to have patience, my king." I giggled to him, hoping to keep him at bay. The laugh must have been convincing enough as he kissed the top of my head before releasing me. I felt a wave of nausea come over me. I moved toward the door as he followed me.

He stepped up beside me to put my arm in his. I forced a smile as he smiled down at me. "I am not used to men being so gallant. Sorry." My plastered fake smile was hurting my cheeks.

"You will get used to it my queen. You are going to have everything your heart desires and more. I will make sure of that."

We walked down the corridor to the main hall as we stood at the landing of the staircase. Everyone in the room bowed to us. We descended the staircase to the open area that was now decorated with all of the lights and greenery, making a beautiful scene. I swallowed hard as I received looks of empathy from several people in our passing. We arrived at the head of the table; it was like Deja Vue from the night before.

A moment of sadness washed over me as the death of Kylan flooded my thoughts. I held back the emotions to play along with the plan.

We were each handed a chalice of wine again as Donis made a toast. "I would like to make a toast to our Goddess and soon to be queen Artemis Natalie. Our nuptials will take place tonight on the Lunar eclipse, blood moon." He turned toward me as he held out the same ring box and ring that Kylan had offered to me. I instantly felt sick. I swallowed hard to keep the bile from rising up and out of my stomach.

My tears started to fall as I nodded my head yes. He put the ring on my finger as he held my hand up for all to see. My tears were of sadness not happiness. I hoped he wouldn't be able to tell the difference. "You are so quiet my queen. I do have a gift for you though." He leaned down to kiss me as I turned my cheek to him. "I do sense some reservation from you." He whispered with anger in his voice.

"I have a gift for the queen, for our upcoming nuptials." He motioned to the men at the back of the room. "Everyone please sit and relax, enjoy the meal. The gift will be here soon."

We sat down as he held my hand tightly in his. "You will do better to remember you will always do as your king wishes Natalie. We can have this the easy nice way or the difficult painful way. Choose wisely."

A plate of food was sat in front of me as I had lost my appetite. I used my fork to move the food around the plate as I feigned to eat. I knew if any food entered my stomach that I would not be able to keep it down.

The doors opened as Collum and the Lycan's brought in Aaron and the other wolves from the pack. They stood just inside the doors of the castle.

Everyone stopped eating to look up as the double doors opened. Most of the people in the crowd gasped with their entrance. The room became deathly silent as Donis released my hand to stand. I stayed in my seat as I didn't know what I should do at this point.

Chapter Eighteen

Carry On

The crowd stood as Donis walked away from his chair to go around the table. He walked with purpose as he glanced over his shoulder at me several times. Watching for some kind of reaction. I sat stoic like nothing was happening. Inside my mind, I was screaming.

Donis was in front of the pack of wolves. His face is grave and serious. "I take it that you have come here to rescue your mate wolf. Well, I hate to tell you that there is no rescuing someone who doesn't need to be rescued. You see, Goddess Artemis Natalie is to become queen of the Lycan's. Her proper place with her royal blood."

He walked a circle around the pack
as he continued. "I think you may want to
check that pretty little neck of hers for the
mark of the king. She is now Lycan, my man.
You should have licked your wounds and
stayed at home." His path led him to be
back directly in front of Aaron.

"You may be the king, but not
rightfully. You can't kill the king and expect
to step up and not have any consequences.
You set up that attack and you were the
one to kill the king to ascend to the title.
How did it feel to kill your king?" Aaron
continued to stare into his eyes that flared
with anger.

"It was actually easier than you think
to surprise the king while he was over there
drooling over who was meant to be my
queen. I knew it from the moment I laid
eyes on her. She is mine, not yours, and not
his." He smoothed his hair back again as he
stood there realizing what he just said.

Gasps came from the other Lycans in
the room, standing at the table. The Lycan
guards had heard what they needed to. The
confession of Donis killing the king.

Aaron stood taller, more proud. His
hands came from behind him that had been
bound, at least thought. "It was easier to
fool you than we thought it would be. You
don't smell the queen on me? I have

marked and mated Natalie as my mate and Luna."

Donis whipped his head around to look at me as he instantly shifted into his Lycan, bounding over everything to capture me in his arms. His Lycan form was larger than I anticipated. Nobody was going to manhandle me this way. I let Kyra come forward to shift. Donis didn't expect me to shift at that moment. A large white wolf stood there snarling at Donis.

That must have been the queue with the rest of the wolves and Lycans to jump into action. The long decorated beautiful table went tumbling across the white tile with a racket as the other Lycans that had been sitting at the table shifted as well.

Donis leaped onto my back with all of the distraction to put his mouth around my throat. Jax and all of the others stopped as they noticed that Donis threatened to rip my throat out. Jax growled in anger as he looked me in the eyes with sadness.

The link came through. "You are my girl, you are strong. I love you." I felt the rumble come from the muzzle of Donis as he heard what Aaron said to me. I took that moment to remember all of my self-defense training. I rolled with enough force to hit Donis against the wall, his teeth dragging across my neck in the motion.

Before I had the time to stand up
the Lycans had swarmed around Donis,
restraining him. The silver collar forced him
to return to his human form. He yelled in
anger and pain from the silver. His eyes
flashed with rage toward Jax.

I stood there in shock that my
maneuver actually worked as the blood
dripped from my neck where his fangs had
scraped me. Jax jumped forward to me as
he knocked me over. I was stunned for a
moment. The look in his eyes was pure love.
He licked the wounds on my neck as I lay
there giggling. The tickle of his tongue sent
sparks throughout my body.

My wounds healed instantly as Jax
licked them. The shivers took over my body
from the sensations he brought me. He
backed up for me to get up off the floor and
stop making an idiot of myself giggling.

As I stood from the floor, the crowd
of people, Lycans and wolves alike bowed

to me. I was stunned by the actions of the people. I had no idea why they would bow to me. I was not the Lycan queen nor the wolf Luna.

I realize that a strange glow surrounds me. The scar on my neck was a bright blue as were my eyes. Jax came to sit next to my side. "You are the true Goddess Artemis, Natalie." I glanced over to the painting or the goddess to notice what I had not before. Her star on her neck and her eyes of bright blue.

The massive painting of the Moon Goddess hung at the landing of the staircase. The beautiful golden-haired Goddess was surrounded in a white glow. The room was flooded with the red glow of the lunar eclipse. The blood moon was at its highest point.

The pulse of white light behind the crowd drew the attention from the eclipse. I turned to see the Moon Goddess standing on the landing of the staircase. I felt the pulse of power fill my body as I bowed to her. "You have no reason to bow to me Goddess, Natalie. We are equals." She seemed to float down the staircase as she stood to the side of Jax.

The crowd was kneeling with her approach. The glow never left her. The beautiful smile of the Moon Goddess calmed all. "Please stand. I am here with the lunar eclipse and the appointment of the new Lycan King. Collum will you please step forward?" She extended her hand out for him.

"You have shown true loyalty to the kingdom and your people. You are to be the reigning king of the Lycans." She placed her hand on the top of his head as he bowed down to her. "You, Collum, are now of royal blood. May the bloodline of the king continue."

The Moon Goddess turned back to me with a beautiful smile. "My dear Natalie. You are the true Goddess Artemis reincarnate. You possess her likeness and powers. You are able to choose if you are to remain a Lycan queen with Collum or return to the human realm with your wolf mate. You are blessed with love in any choice you make."

I looked immediately at Jax. His eyes searched mine for the answer he sought. "My wolf mate had rejected me out of misunderstanding." Jax bowed his head. "I would like that to be revoked." Jax's head came up quickly as a tear left his eye. "I choose to remain with my fated wolf mate."

"All has been revoked of his rejection at your request, Goddess. You are now the bridge between the Lycan and wolves. As a Goddess you are immortal in the Lycan realm. If you choose your wolf mate to be immortal as well, you have the ability to mark him and share the power you have."

Collum turned to all of the Lycans to have them bow to him, as their new king. With the outpouring of support, the Moon Goddess was gone as quickly as she had arrived. "Please get robes for our wolf allies." Collum asked the crowd.

Several people had gone and returned with robes for the wolves to shift back to their human form. Aaron and the others shifted back into their human form, putting the robes on.

I stood frozen as I didn't know what I should do. My body stood still as my mind yelled to go to Aaron. Finally my body and mind connected for me to move from my spot.

The comforting arms of Aaron wrapped around my body as our lips met in a need that consumed both of us. I pulled my head back to look at him again. "Are you sure you are okay? You aren't hurt are you?"

"I am fine, my Luna. I take it you will marry me now my Goddess? I love you more than the moon and stars in the sky. I am yours."

I leaned over to whisper in his ear. "You can say, mine, when we are in bed. I will allow that." I pulled back smiling as he kissed my neck lovingly.

Chapter Nineteen

Decision to Love

I heard the Great Wall of China falling like a stack of bricks. One by one the chain reaction started. I cringe inside with every echo that shakes me. The earthquake from within shook me to the core.

The decision was made to stay at the castle for the night, leaving at first light. Aaron and I were shown to the visitors chambers. Collum was going to be a great king. He knew that he had more allies then they had ever had. King Collum had it written in the history books of the events that took place in the castle during the week.

Collum made sure that Aaron and I knew that it was to be written in the archives that we were welcome to reside in the realm if we so chose for the immortality of the Goddess and the mate of her choice.

Aaron and I bowed to King Collum prior to retiring to our chambers for the night. "You are never to bow to anyone, Goddess. You are the distinguished guest of any realm." Collum then bowed to me in return.

"Thank you for everything, Collum. Jax and I owe you for helping us. If you should ever need us, please send word. You are always welcome within my home as well." He extended his hand for the king. Collum shook his hand with a smile.

"If you should need anything while here, please don't hesitate to ask. We are here for every whim of the Goddess Natalie." I smiled to him sweetly as I wrapped my arms around his neck in appreciation. "Please don't get Jax jealous. He is a bit of a handful." He laughed as he kissed me on the cheek. We heard the growl come from within Aaron. "There you are Jax." He chuckled again as he turned to walk away.

Aaron's arms wrapped around my waist as the groan emanated from his chest. "It's fine Jax. No other man is going to take your place." I giggled as Aaron backed up to the doors, kicking them open to a room that was as nice as the king's chambers.

"Now exactly where were we earlier?" Aaron spins me in place to face him. He stood there looking down into my eyes.

I pull away, running to the other side of the bed. "I have no idea what you are talking about." I grin sideways at him as he comes around the bed after me. I got across the bed just in time as he got to the spot I had stood. "Looks like I win this one."

"You only wish. Now stop moving. I have some catching up to do with you. No fancy maneuvers on me either missy." He chuckled like he was having fun with the chase.

I faked a move the other direction as we both met in the center of the bed. He rotated his body so that I was on his chest when we landed.

"That was pretty slick. you know. You will have to teach me that move." I grinned.

"I have no problem teaching you a move that lands me on top of you." He laughed as he placed both hands around my face to kiss me with the passion I felt for him with our bodies touching. My core was already tightening with the anticipation of what was promised.

Aaron tugged my dress up and over my head as I lay there naked on top of him. "So much better." He groaned, possessing my mouth again. His hands slid down my body slowly.

I reached down between us to untie his robe. Pushing the fabric to the sides. "Now that, is so much better." The feel of our skin touching lit a fire that only his body could put out.

He rolled us over so that he could take his robe off each arm with my help. Kissing him was like feeling everything on my lips that I craved. His weight on my body took my breath away at the feel. He kissed my neck with his mark and growled with passion.

His lips and tongue worked their way to my breasts one by one. My hard nipples ached for his hot wet mouth as his hand pulled my leg to the side more, opening my core to his touch. His hand covered my core for a moment before his skilled hand found my clit to rub as he slid his hand back and forth to feel my hot wet core aching for him.

My hands wandered his muscular arms and shoulders as his mouth covered my core with his tongue rubbing over my clit to make my body arch into his. My hands filled with his hair as the tension in my core built to exploding. I moved my hips as he made my body spasm again and again.

He came up my body again as I regained some control again. I placed both hands over his chest to feel the solid muscles. I watched as his muscles twitched with every touch. I traced over several tattoos as I admired the patch of hair on his chest that led down his stomach to the object of my desire at the moment.

I traced the path of hair down over his abdomen as he held himself above me. My fingers made their way down the ripples of muscles on his stomach as he twitched with my touch. I savored in the feel of his skin on my fingertips, the sounds he made as I moved my fingers with feathery touches. "You are killing me Nat. You are driving me to the brink of madness." He sucked in his breath as I ran my fingers down the length of his shaft. The tip wet with desire as I wrapped my hand around the thickness to feel the velvet skin. I continued to touch him for a few more moments before he let out a growl that I felt as much as heard.

"Madness is only a breath away for me right now my goddess." He pressed his lips to mine for a tender yet demanding kiss. I returned the passion in my kiss as I wrapped my arms and legs around his body. I felt him tremble as I tightened my legs around his hips. His hand guided him to my core. As he entered me the sensations ran through my veins like electricity in my veins.

Aaron had his mouth on mine the entire time, slowly pushing my body to its limits. He threw his head back as his body was connected to mine in pleasure. He relaxed his body more with mine. I moved my hips just enough to cause him to moan in pleasure.

"You think so, do you?" He picked me up pushing my body against the velvet headboard as he was on his knees. He grabbed hold of the headboard behind me as he moved with purpose as I ran my fingernails down his back. I didn't think he could go any deeper, but he did. As I was straddling his lap, I sank further down onto him.

His movements made me move on him as he thrust into me slowly. The tightening of my core made me move more. I rocked my hips in motion with his. I pushed my pelvis forward as he leaned into me. The perfect amount of pressure to have my body melt with the surges in my core. I started to scream as his mouth came down on mine.

"You are mine. I want to claim you again. Please Nat."

"Yes Aaron, yes." Is all that my mind could muster at the time.

My head rolled to the side as his teeth sank into my flesh to cause me to orgasm again as he growled into my ear. The vibration from his body caused me to scream in ecstasy. His body finally calmed from the spasms as he retracted his teeth.

He slumped over my body with his head on the headboard next to mine. "Oh my goddess. The things you do to me. You have no idea. I have never felt anything so intense in all of my life. We were definitely made to be together." His breathing was slowing as I took the opportunity to run my hands over his body even more. His skin was like a drug that I craved. I couldn't get enough of touching him.

"You might need to give me a minute after that one, my goddess. I can't believe I just said that. I didn't think that was possible." He sat back on his heels to put his hands around my face. He looked through my eyes to my soul. "Will you marry me, my goddess? Make me the happiest man in the world forever. I devote my heart and soul to you and Kyra."

I sat there with our bodies still connected. I said nothing for a few seconds. I wondered how long he would wait before he would blow up and pop. "On one condition."

"Anything, you name it. You want the moon; I will give it to you. If you want the stars, I will gather them up for you." He smiled so sweetly that I melted even more.

"I get to claim you so we can be together forever if we choose." I didn't break my gaze from his eyes.

"Claim away my goddess. You can bite me anytime. I like how you react to my bite. If it's anything like that for me, I'm down." He laughed, placing a kiss on my lips. "So, that's a yes?"

"Yes." I returned his kiss again with another.

"Tomorrow we will go home and let them know the good news. She finally gave in to me. I wore her down." He started laughing as I bit his neck. "Ouch, that hurt a little." He chuckled again.

"I love you so much. You make me happy and Jax is purring like a little kitten. He has never been this happy. Jax will decide eventually that he wants you and Kyra. There won't be much stopping him then." He chuckled as I giggled at him.

"I love you too Aaron. I didn't think I would ever say those words to anybody ever again. I don't know how you did it, but you did."

Chapter Twenty

Going Home

The suns rose just over the horizon as I stretched out my sore muscles. I was sore in all of the right ways. We made love again during the night. I curled up into the arms of Aaron for the rest of the night to sleep soundly, not dreaming.

Aaron opened his eyes to smile at me as I stretched. "Sore honey? You may walk a little funny today. Every step will remind you that you belong with me." He kissed me as he climbed over me. He walked to the bathroom. The view was incredible for me. I don't think I will ever get enough of what this man can do to me.

I walked to the bathroom to hear the shower running. "You were going to shower without me?"

"Hell no honey. I was coming out to get you. I can't allow you to shower alone. That's one of the rules of a relationship. Always shower together, or at least I watch you shower." He grinned as he picked me up in his arms, carrying me into the shower with him.

The shower felt amazing on my muscles. The hot water cascaded over my body to help limber the muscles some. We would have a trip back to the pack today. I needed my muscles for more than satisfying our needs.

King Collum met us downstairs in the main hall when we were ready. "You slept well I hope." Grinning at us. "After all of the commotion anyway." I felt my blush from my face to my toes. Aaron just grinned from ear to ear.

The other wolves from the pack laughed with the comment. "Better watch out guys. She can open quite a can of kick ass on you. She has taken me down before."

"Don't worry, we will remember that until the day we die, watching her take you down." The laughter broke out then the men seemed to realize they were talking to Aaron again. "Sorry, no disrespect meant." He cleared his throat and turned to the other men.

"It is time that we head for home King Collum. We will return another time. Let us know when we have something else to celebrate. Better yet, we will have you

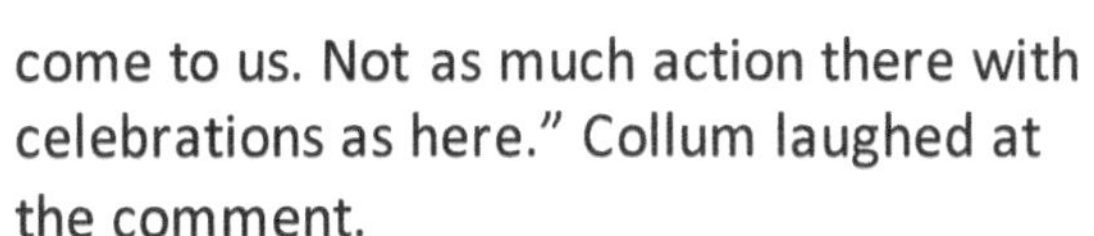

come to us. Not as much action there with celebrations as here." Collum laughed at the comment.

I spoke to Collum then. "I have met with the healers here, leaving some of my blood for you to use as needed. If you need me though, please don't hesitate to send word." I reached up to give him a hug. Jax didn't growl this time.

"Safe trip. If you need anything please let us know. I would love to attend your wedding."

"You will be among the first to be invited." Aaron extended his hand to Collum. "Thank you for everything."

"Our goddess." The group of Lycan's knelt down before we walked out the door. I thanked them all for the hospitality, protection, and understanding.

We walked to the realm portal to our world. As we went through the portal I felt the sadness of Kalen come over me one last time. "I know you don't want to hear about another man, but I wanted to let you know that I do understand why you rejected me like you did." The other wolves went into the trees to undress to shift into their wolves.

"I was also mated to King Kalen. I watched him die and I felt the pain that you spoke about. I know the pain you felt with me now. I just wanted you to know that I do understand now."

Aaron grabbed me into his arms, holding me close to himself. "I'm sorry you had to go through that too, my love. I would never wish that on anyone." He kissed my forehead. "I am happy that you have chosen me though. I hope I can make up for him as well. I can't blame him for loving you."

I pulled back to look up into his eyes as a tear trailed down my face. He wiped the tear from my face, replacing it with a kiss. "I love you Natalie, let's go home now."

Aaron stripped down right there in front of me. I watched him in all of his glory as he shifted. I was the last to shift. The other pack members still watched me in awe after my shift.

We took off at a steady sprint toward home. Aaron linked to John to let him know we were back, and they had me with them. As we got to the boundaries of the property I sensed something was wrong. I stopped as we got to the tree edge from the pack house.

Aaron stopped as I did. "Aaron, something is wrong? I feel it just like the night that King Kalen was murdered. I can't tell you what is wrong, just that something is wrong." I looked around frantically as I tried to figure out why I had this feeling. We stood there together for a little bit as we waited to see if something was going to happen.

Nothing happened. We stood there for at least ten minutes. I linked to John. "Is everything ok John? We are almost home."

"Things are fine here. Why do you ask? You guys just get home." Aaron tilted his head up letting out the melodious howl for the pack to know they were coming. We waited for a couple of minutes before the return howl came.

"John took his time with that one." Aaron was ready to be home.

"Please everyone be careful. I can't shake the feeling that something is wrong though." I rubbed along Jax to let him know I loved him. The other wolves sprinted off toward the pack house as we trotted along behind them. They had missed their families while they were gone. Excited to see them.

We get to the steps of the pack house as all of the wolves shift back into their human forms. I delayed my shift for a few minutes with my senses in overdrive that something was not right. I watched and listened closely. There were no families waiting for our return like when we came back the last time. Where was everyone?

"Natalie, why are you waiting to shift back? Do you still have a strange feeling?"

I mind linked to Aaron. "Where are all of the people? Why is no one here with our return?"

Aaron looked around as his face paled at the realization that something was different. Just as he was to respond to me men came from all directions with nets made of silver. I heard a growl come from Aaron, but it was too late. The net settled over his body as he yelled in pain. I tried to remove the net with my jaws, but the pain was too much.

"Run Natalie, run. Don't let them catch you." Aaron struggled to get the words out with the pain he was enduring. The black rogue wolf that had attacked us before lunged at me. I was able to move away just in time.

I needed to get away to come up with a plan to help the pack. I couldn't help them if I were captured as well. I howled in pain as I ran for the tree line. The wolves came after me, but I was much larger and faster than they were. I ended up losing them just outside of the boundaries of the pack. The pain of leaving the pack cut like a knife through my heart.

The darkness consumed the forest as the sun descended behind the mountains. I had to get somewhere that I could think. I needed a plan. If I went back to the realm of the Lycan's I would use up so much precious time. I needed someone closer. Someone just as strong.

I came to a small clearing with the mountainside along the clearing. A rock formation halfway up the mountain proved to be a place to not be seen, but the advantage of seeing someone coming. I walked in the water to not leave a scent to follow. My brain was not functioning at full capacity right now.

I entered the rock formation. I kept in my wolf form, to move faster and I would be stronger. I curled up missing Aaron and Jax for comfort. Kyra decided to stay alert as I slept and thought about what the plan was going to be to rescue everyone in the pack.

The meadow came into my view as I scanned the area. I was obviously in a dream right now. The silence in the meadow helped my mind to function better. I wish that Nana were here to help me through this. I always thought out loud to Nana, coming up with a solution.

Nana yelled out from my right. I ran to her. The embrace of Nana always helped to make things better. "I told you that I was always here when you needed me. I have missed you dear."

Nana, I have a major problem. Someone has taken Aaron and all of the pack hostage. I have no idea who it is, what they want. Or if everyone is okay. Aaron pleaded with me to run. I feel like such a coward." I covered my face as my tears escaped from my eyes.

"You are not a coward my dear. You are the strongest, wisest person I know. We will get this figured out."

"I ran though while everyone else was captured."

"My dear girl, you did the wise thing. You can now get the help you need to get them back."

"I don't have the time to get to the Lycan realm to get help. It is too far."

"What do you mean? The portal is right here. You can go right now to the realm of the Lycan's. You will be entering into the king's dreams, but he will hear you."

I entered the portal of the realm to call King Collum for help. I linked to his dream. "The rogue's that had attacked us before have captured everyone but me. I need help as quickly as possible please. There are no less than ten wolves with the rogue's."

"We are on the way, my Goddess. We will meet you by the boundaries of your pack. I will send extra reinforcements. It will only take us a couple of hours to make it to you. Stay safe my Goddess."

I stepped back through the portal to no one being there with me. Nana had helped me again. I yelled out, "I love you Nana." I

Kyra alerted me that we were not alone. There was another wolf coming nearer to us. I listened and watched for any changes. I heard the sniffle of a child, then a sob. I sniffed the air again to recognize the scent of little Luke.

"Luke, where are you? It's the white wolf, Natalie. I am mind linking to you buddy." I listen carefully for his reply to me verbally. The sound of his little scared voice comes from the left. I step out another step to see him stumbling around in the dark. He doesn't have a wolf yet. He is too young. I step out one more step as he notices my white fur. He comes running to me, wrapping his arms around my neck.

I looked around again to make sure that no one had followed him or used him as bait for me. I curl up tucking Luke into my middle to keep him warm. "What happened Luke? Where is your mother?"

"The bad wolves came and took mommy. I was playing in the treehouse. Mommy did the finger over the lips at me to be quiet. I listened to my mommy. I hid there until everyone was gone. I don't know

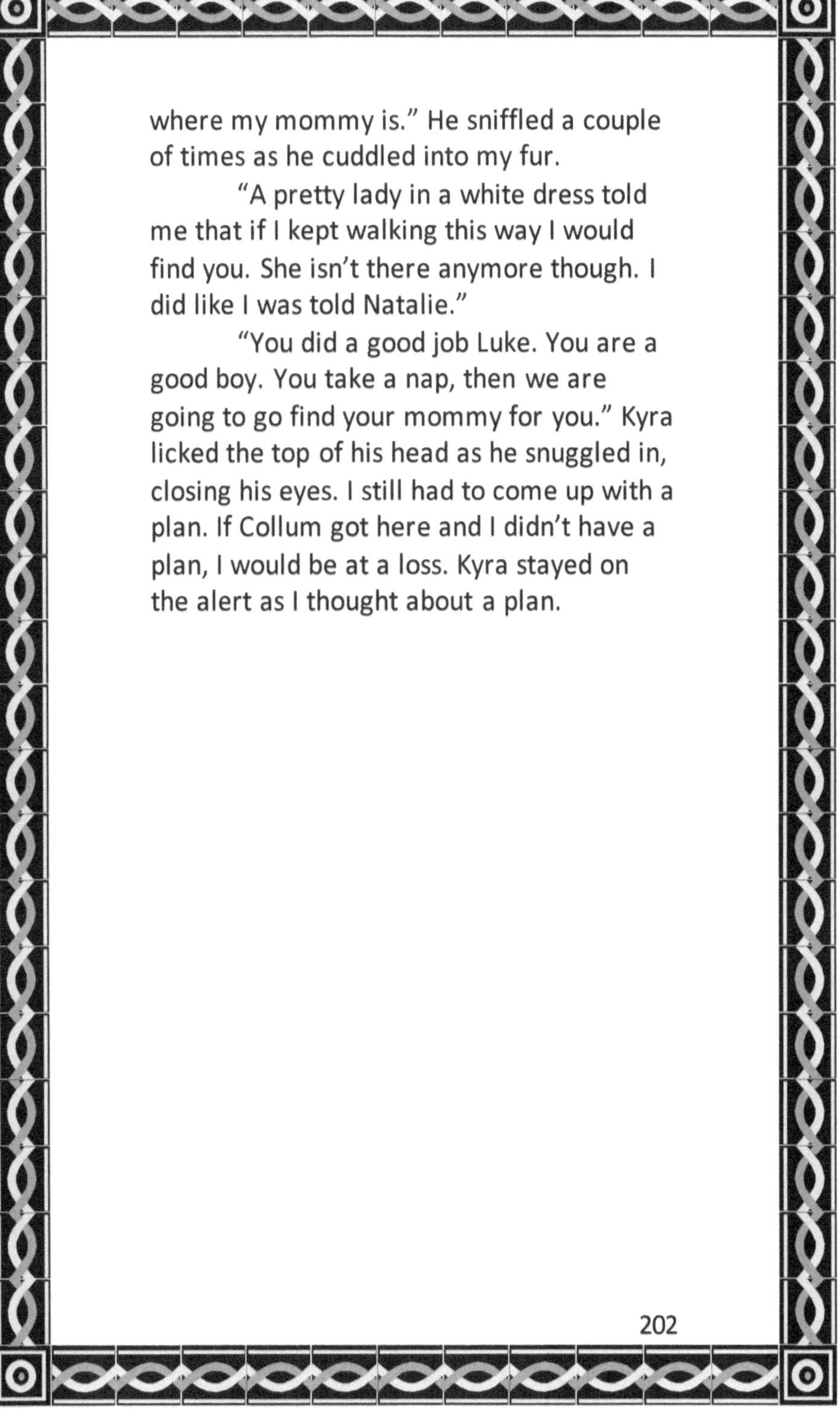

where my mommy is." He sniffled a couple
of times as he cuddled into my fur.

"A pretty lady in a white dress told
me that if I kept walking this way I would
find you. She isn't there anymore though. I
did like I was told Natalie."

"You did a good job Luke. You are a
good boy. You take a nap, then we are
going to go find your mommy for you." Kyra
licked the top of his head as he snuggled in,
closing his eyes. I still had to come up with a
plan. If Collum got here and I didn't have a
plan, I would be at a loss. Kyra stayed on
the alert as I thought about a plan.

Chapter Twenty-One

For You, My Love

The time came for us to move to the boundaries to meet with Collum. I packed Luke on my back. I made sure he could hang on. I told him that no matter what he was to stay on my back. If for some reason he fell off to run and keep running. He understood his directions. He clung to my back for dear life.

We were hidden in the trees as Collum and at least twenty other Lycan's approached us. The cavalry had arrived. Luke was scared at first as he had never seen a Lycan. I told them they were our friends.

I went over my plan with Collum that didn't agree with my decision but nodded to me in acknowledgement. I sent a link to Aaron. "Aaron can you hear me?" I knew that the wolves could hear our link.

Aaron replied, "don't you even think about it my goddess. I love." The link was stopped.

The Lycan's all took their positions as I told Luke to go ahead and let go now. "I need you to stay right here. You don't leave this spot unless I tell you to run. You will run that way." I pointed in the other direction. Luke shook his head yes to me. He hugged me one more time as I walked out of the tree line into the clearing outside of the pack houses. I could see the wolves that surrounded the area.

I continued to walk toward the pack house. The wolves were not familiar to me. I knew they were with the rogue. I looked at each as I walked by. I snarled in warning to each that I meant business. I walked slowly with purpose as I approached the pack house stairs.

I stopped at the bottom of the stairs. Kyra looked around at the other wolves with her teeth bared, snarling. A middle-aged man walked out of the doors of the house that looked like Aaron but older. How can that be?

The man laughed as he walked to the edge of the porch. "I see you are special. You are the white wolf that I long for. I almost had you once, but you were more capable than I thought. Now I know how capable you are though."

I opened a mind link for all to hear. "Who are you? What do you want?"

"No chance of you shifting to human then? You are going to continue to stay your wolf. I heard you have something special. I decided the one that controls that something special is going to be a very rich and respected man."

"First of all. No man controls me. Not even an alpha. Have you spoken with Aaron by chance? Where is he? He will tell you that no man controls me." I seethed with anger to rip out his throat.

He took a step toward me as the saliva dripped from Kyra's jowls with her snap and snarl. "Calm down my dear. I will not hurt you. You have something very precious I want."

"Well I will hurt you if you don't start talking. I asked you a question."

One of the wolves jumped at me as I was able to jump up grabbing him by the throat, crushing his windpipe instantly. I dropped the wolf at my feet as I prepared for another attack.

"Where is Aaron and the rest of the pack?" I snarled with my eyes glowing a bright green now. "I want my questions answered and I am not a patient person."

"Let me tell you a little story first. Then we will talk shop more. We do need alpha Aaron out here though. He will like this story too." He motioned to a man standing in the doorway.

The man came out with Aaron handcuffed with silver behind his back. His shirt had blood spatter on it, his lip was bruised as well as his eye. I saw red as I looked to Aaron. I saw him mouth the words; I love you.

"Well, now we can have story time. Are you listening too Aaron? It's a boy. Those are the words I should have heard. Your dear daddy, Derek." Aaron looked up at him with confusion. "Dear daddy Derek was my twin brother. I am Devin. Shocker of the year." Aaron looked at him with shock.

"Dear daddy Derek and I were to be the reigning alphas. We had been given a mate as all are. However, Derek didn't want to share a mate with me. He was always an asshole. Am I not right Aaron?" He ran his hand through his hair.

"Anyway. I wanted to keep our mate, but it came down to what Derek wanted. Our mate was rejected and left. Somehow, some way, we were blessed to get a second chance mate. Your beautiful mother Maurine. Derek decided he didn't want her, but I chose to keep her. I wasn't going to let another mate be rejected by Derek. The problem was, Derek abused

Maurine. She was normally with me." He moved back and forth on the porch now.

"The good part of the story is coming. Maurine found out she was pregnant. Derek wanted an heir as any alpha, but he damn good and well that the baby was not his. Now for the good part, are you ready? I am your father Aaron. Devin, not Derek. He left her alone during her pregnancy. I loved your mother. I really did. When it was about time for you to be born, Derek decided he didn't want anyone to know that I was the father of her baby."

Aaron's look of confusion made my heart hurt for him. He is finding out that his life has been a lie.

"Derek decided there could only be one alpha in the pack. He had some of the pack members take me out to kill me. Well they didn't kill me as you can see. I barely lived. I was taken in by a woman in another pack that nursed me back to health. Before I recovered I found out that Maurine had died in childbirth. I think the bastard actually killed her."

A tear slid down Aaron's cheek with the story of his mother and the fact that the man whom he thought was his father was not.

"I have waited and watched as you have become who you are now. I watched you become Derek all over again. You don't deserve to have a woman as special as the goddess. The night Derek died I thought about stepping forward to retain my rightful spot within the pack. I had to go through the pain of losing the first mate we were given, your mother Natalie. She was taken from me and with her death came the pain of the loss again. I suppose I may have gone mad for a while after that."

He looked at me with sadness in his eyes. I saw the pain that he endured not once but actually three times. That would be enough to drive any person insane. I almost felt sorry for him.

"So, the end of story time. I am ready for my chance to have the love, respect, and money that I deserve now. I can have all of that with you Natalie."

"What do you want from me?" I snarled at him.

"It is simple my dear Goddess Natalie. If you come with me, I will let them all go about their lives once again. I will release everyone. I want you my dear, to put it simply."

"You know that I have a mate bond with Aaron. I would never be able to love you."

"Aaron has already rejected you my dear goddess. All you have to do now is to simply reject him. Then you are free to love whomever you choose. That is the reason you left the first time, is it not? I know all of these little things."

I swallowed hard at the thought of rejecting Aaron. I had thought at one time that it was the answer to everything. I came to realize why he did what he did and now when I actually decide to love someone, I am supposed to let them go. I am willing to do what I must to have Aaron safe though.

Aaron looked at me with glassy eyes. His tears threatened to spill at the thought of me rejecting him. I knew I had no choice.

I chose to shift to my human form to make everything easier. I stood there in front of the steps as I looked into Devin's face. "Now that I am in human form, I will go with you, but I want you to let everyone go now. If you refuse, then no deal."

"Let them all go to their homes then I will reject him."

Devin motioned to the men at the door to let everyone leave. The people of the pack walked out, bowing their heads to me as they walked by. Aaron continued to hang his head as he stood there, handcuffed.

All of the pack members had come out. John stood by my side. "I stay with my Goddess. No matter where she goes."

"So be it. You will be loyal to me, or you will die a slow painful death." Devin stepped down the stairs as I stepped back a couple steps. He approached me slowly. I stopped as we were just away from the stairs.

"I want all of your pack here, now. I don't want any tricks." I demanded as he started to circle around me.

"You are a demanding little thing, aren't you? You have spirit. I like that in a woman." His path continued around me.

"You aren't going to like that spirit much if I don't get what I want." I stood taller with my chin up.

His path stopped directly behind me as he linked to his pack to come to the pack house immediately. I felt the lightest of touches as he touched my hair. I stood as a statue to not react. He continued his path to my side as the other pack members made their way to the pack house.

One of his pack walks up holding Luke in his arms, squirming. "He says he is with the white wolf Natalie. He was in the tree line."

"Well isn't that sweet. I know you don't have any children. Oh yes, he is the boy that you saved." He took Luke from the other man as Luke hit at him.

"Calm down Luke. I want you to release Aaron and give Luke to him." I think he saw the fear in my eyes now. I have never been good at hiding my feelings. My face usually says it all.

"Tell you what my Goddess. I will let alpha Aaron go but I think I am going to hold on to this little guy until you are finished here. When you are done, I will let Aaron have him." He gave me a quick fake smile.

"I Natalie Harmon reject you alpha Aaron Meyers as my alpha and mate. I accept your rejection." I looked into Aaron's eyes as the hurt took over his body. He fell to his knees as the man removed the silver handcuffs.

I turned to Devin, reaching for Luke. "I will take him to Aaron now. I did what I said I was going to do."

"You have kept your end of the bargain." He handed Luke to me.

I stepped up onto the steps as the first wave of Lycan's appeared from the shadows to surround the wolf pack. The wolves looked around in confusion as the Lycan's surrounded them.

"You sly little vixen. You had this planned the entire time. I underestimated you." Devin stood there staring at me.

"Never mess with a woman on a mission. I told you that you obviously didn't know much about me. Did you really think I was going to let my pack suffer? Or the man I love?"

"You just rejected him though. I guess you didn't realize that I had his rejection to me voided. I can fix this problem. I have the power to choose my mate. My bond remains with alpha Aaron." I stood tall with a straight back as the Lycan's rounded up Devin's pack.

Chapter Twenty-Two

Redemption

I sat Luke down as I turned my attention to Aaron. I fell to my knees in front of him, holding his face and kissing him. "I'm so sorry you had to go through that. I had to do it to save everyone." Aaron looked up to me with the pain leaving his face, little by little.

"I, Goddess Natalie of the Waning Moon pack hereby accept you, alpha Aaron Meyers as my alpha and mate. For eternity." I smiled at Aaron as his pain left his eyes and face.

"Just so you know, this may hurt a little. I don't know for sure what I am doing." I kissed the right side of his neck as he moved his head for me. My fangs protruded as I sank my teeth into his neck. I felt a surge of power go through my veins. Aaron felt it to as he wrapped his arms around me. I withdrew my teeth from his skin to feel the tingle of the mixture of our blood.

I whisper into his ear. "Now the fun part. I get to mate you later. It's your turn now." I tilted my head to the side. "I love you my Goddess Natalie," whispered, his lips feathering across my skin. His teeth sank into my neck over the scar to make my body yearn for more of him.

"Natalie, I want you to know how sorry I am that I rejected you. The pain is horrible. I will spend the rest of my life trying to make it up to you."

"You know you will because now you are the chosen by the Goddess for immortality with me. You aren't going anywhere."

"I really hate to break this up, but I would like you to know that we have Devin and his pack all secured and ready to leave now. They will stand a trial." Collum spoke like a true king as he stood there smiling and shaking his head at us.

I got up and ran to Collum to wrap my arms around his neck to say thank you for the help. "We honestly didn't do anything, Goddess. It was your strength and true Luna instincts that made this possible. We just provided the muscle, per say." He chuckled as he hugged me back.

"I am eternally grateful for your help again Collum. We really need to stop meeting under these pretenses."

"I completely agree. I will expect an invitation to the upcoming wedding. By the way, I haven't heard Jax growl at me in quite a while. He leaned down, kissing me on the cheek. The rumble came from Jax. "There you are my friend." Collum laughed fully as he turned, walking away.

Aaron's wrists were raw and burnt as I took his hands in mine. "I wish I could help to make this feel better."

"I will live with these as long as I have you. I may need you to kiss them better later though. By the way, how did you get them here so quickly?"

"I have my ways." I smiled sideways to his grin. "I am still learning too."

"Luke, I want you to go straight home to your mother now. No stopping or playing along the way. Your poor mother is probably worried sick about you right now. Can you be a big boy for me and do that?"

"Yes my Luna. I will have to tell mommy the whole story of how you saved me again." Luke hugged me before he hurried off to his house. "I love you."

"I see other men worship you as much as I do." Aaron wrapped his arms around me, leaning over to place a kiss on my neck.

"Are you up for a shower?" I smile at the words as Aaron sucks in his breath.

"You don't have to ask me twice. I haven't seen you naked yet today. Only if I get to wash your hair though." Aaron laughed as he swept me up into his arms.

I snuggled into his chest as he carried me up to my room. I could definitely get used to this. Never thought I would.

Before I could get completely undressed Aaron had the shower running, stepping in waiting for me. I chuckled and shook my head as I admired the view.

After our shower I got dressed into a nice outfit of a floral top with my jeans and of course sandals. Aaron came back with a blue button top with his jeans that hugged him in all the right places.

"I am starving. How about you? Let's go have some supper." Aaron laces his fingers through mine as we get to the landing of the staircase to see the entire pack, bowing to us.

"Everyone has gotten together tonight in the great hall to celebrate our Goddess and Luna. The pack is ever so grateful for the actions and bravery of our future Luna today. The feast is ready." John spoke with such confidence and pride.

We descended the stairs for all cheering for our arrival. The great hall's tables were loaded with so much food.

Luke and Ana approached me to personally thank me for saving him in the forest for the night. "I love you white wolf Natalie. You are my Luna aren't you?"

"I love you too Luke. I suppose I am your Luna." I smiled back to his puppy dog eyes while he had his arms wrapped around my leg. I scuffed his hair. "You are such a brave, big boy Luke."

"Your baby will be just like me. I will teach him how to be brave and a good boy for you." I chuckle to him.

"Someday you will make a good friend."

"I mean this baby," putting his hand on my stomach.

I looked at Luke in shock. I had never even thought about the fact that I could be pregnant. I have not had my pills for a while now. I figured I would keep it to myself for now. I didn't know anything other than a little boy with an active imagination making statements.

We finally made our way to the head of the table. We sat down as the pack members all smiled at me in adoration. "I think the pack loves you, my goddess." Aaron whispered into my ear causing me to get goosebumps.

"Can we all stand to make a toast to the Goddess Natalie. I want to thank every one of you for the show of gratitude to Natalie that she deserves with her courage, love, and caring for this pack. As some of you may know, Natalie is new to our world. She has lived in the human world her entire life."

I stood there smiling at all of the faces that smiled to me. The happiness displayed was of epic proportions.

Aaron turned toward me, dropping to a knee holding a box toward me with the most beautiful ring of silver and gold with a large diamond in the middle. The intricate work of vines around the band. "Goddess

Natalie, will you honor me in becoming my wife and the Luna of the Waning Moon pack?"

I stood in shock, as I looked to the crowd that was so silent you could have heard a pin drop. I turn back to Aaron. I feel the heaviness in my chest as the words, "I will," came out of my mouth.

Aaron placed the ring on my finger before standing and giving the pack a show with a kiss that took my breath away. He stood with his forehead on mine. "I love you so much my goddess. I am yours and you are mine. I will cherish you until the end of time."

The cheering of the pack members broke the silence in my head as I smiled at the pack that I was now part of. The love of so many people flooded over me that I couldn't help but to cry. My family has always been so limited. Now I have all of the love that I had missed out on for all of these years.

Chapter Twenty-Three
Happily Ever After

That night we made love several times. I am insatiable with this man. I crave his touch and love. My walls have fallen, and I am happy. Nana was right. Who am I kidding though. Nana was always right. I just wish she were here now to share in the happiness that I have found.

Aaron now snuggled me to his body. His even breathing and steady heartbeat calmed my mind, body, and soul. I drifted off into a blissful sleep.

Walking through the meadow was always so calming and made me happy. I walked along touching all of the flowers with a calmness in my soul. The warm breeze whispered across my face, kissing me with a wisp of hair.

"Nat my dear girl." Nana's voice came from behind me. Next to her, stood a little boy with dark hair and bright blue eyes. He held Nana's hand, smiling at me. "Go ahead, go

to your mommy." Nana released his hand, motioning for him to go.

I fell to my knees in the realization that this was not just any little boy. He was my little boy. His arms wrapped around my neck as I cradled him. My tears of happiness fell. "Hi mommy. I will see you soon." I continued to hold onto him tightly.

I opened my eyes to look at Nana. The happiness of the moment took my breath away as a little girl of blonde hair and green eyes smiled at me, holding Nana's other hand. "Go." Nana released her.

I gathered both of the children in my arms, holding tight to both. My tears of happiness streamed down my face. I hugged them both to me smiling. "I love you little ones. I can't wait to see you again." They both placed a kiss on my cheek, returning to Nana, each grabbing a hand. "I love you too Nana. I miss you every day."

My eyes flew open as I was crying, Aaron wiping my tears. "Nat, what is the matter? Did you have a bad dream?" I sat up to rub my temples.

"Quite the opposite. I met our children. They were with Nana. The little boy was the spitting image of you and the girl was my reflection. They were so sweet. I got to hug on them and even talk to them." I realized the words that just fell out of my mouth in rapid succession, from the look on Aaron's face.

I closed my eyes tight for a moment. Not knowing what else I should say now. I never would have told him that way if I had my choice. I took a deep breath, opening my eyes to Aaron sitting there with a smile on his face, as he put his hand on my stomach.

"Twins?" He looked down to my stomach then back into my eyes. I didn't know what kind of a reaction to expect.

Aaron pushed be back down onto the pillow to possess my lips in the most loving kiss. He came up from the kiss to move to my stomach. He kissed my stomach several times. "I suppose we better get married before you don't fit into a wedding dress. I can't wait to meet our children."

"You are going to have the sexiest baby body ever."

The End

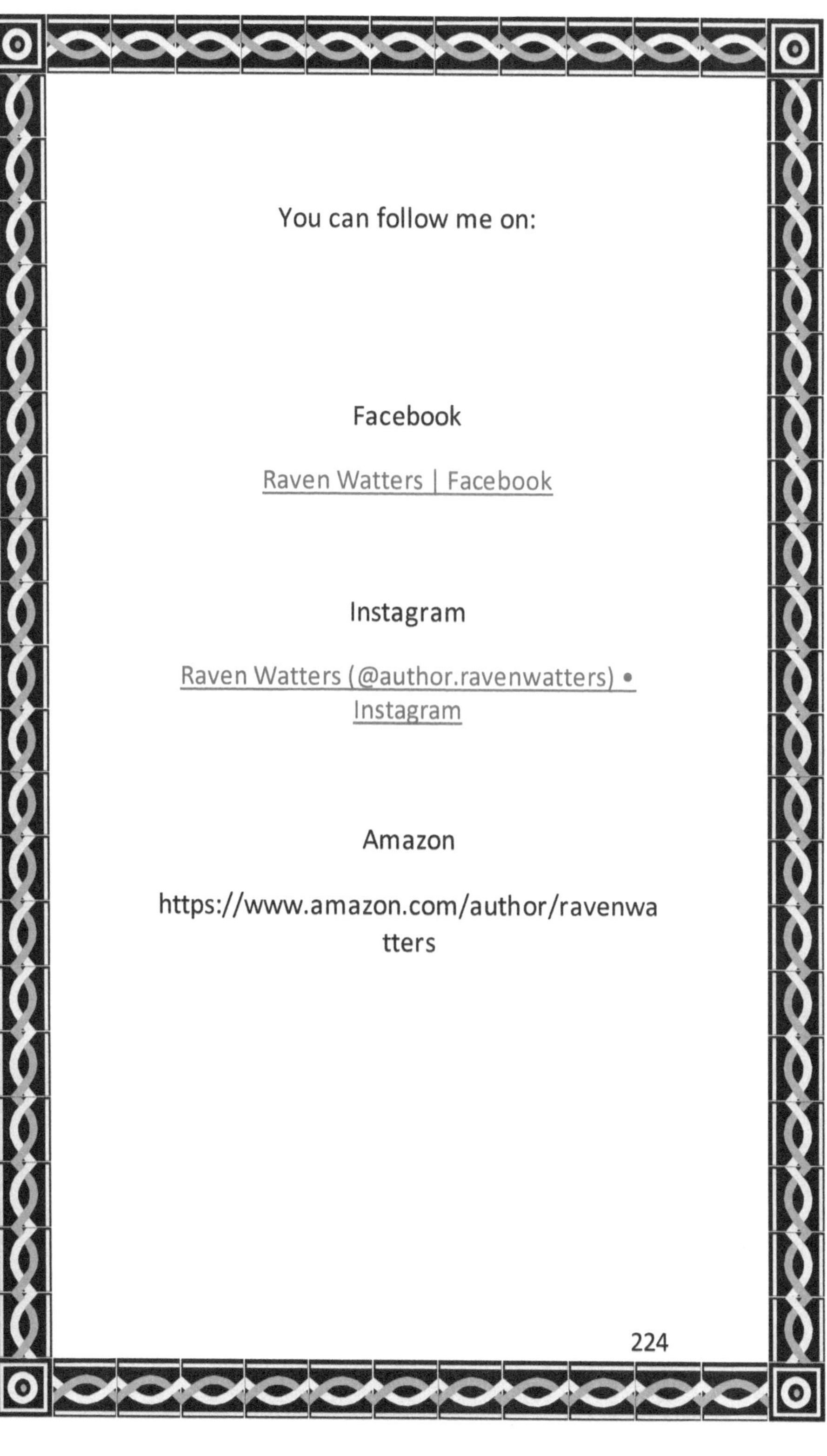

You can follow me on:

Facebook

Raven Watters | Facebook

Instagram

Raven Watters (@author.ravenwatters) • Instagram

Amazon

https://www.amazon.com/author/ravenwatters